MURDER OF
CROWS

A Lake
Pines
Mystery

Lake Pines Mystery Series
Murder At First Light

Death At Deception Bay

Murder Of Crows

The Dead Of Winter

The Night Is Darkest

Conspiracy Of Blood

Anna Ledin Thriller Series
The Blackwater Operative

The Phoenix Code

Rogue

Blown

Teen & Young Adult
Unfollowed

Order From Karoo Bridge

Carole And The Secret Queen's Scarf

Genre Fiction
The Hotel Penn

Our Forgotten Year

The Plus One

MURDER OF CROWS

A gripping Lake Pines Mystery

L.L. Abbott

Paperback ISBN- 978-1-989325-14-8
eBook ISBN 978-1-989325-15-5
Large Print Paperback ISBN 978-1-989325-16-2

To all the people who love a gripping murder mystery with a twist, as well as those that appreciate the intelligence of the crow ~ especially for Drew who loves both.
~ you're the best

And to Kirstin for your friendship + support, even though you oddly read the ending first, you still read every book
~ thanks

MURDER OF CROWS

"Most ancient cultures believe that crows are an omen and can guide humans into the afterlife. Some believe the crow to be sacred and hold mystical powers. All I know is that when there is a murder of crows around you, you need to leave, because it either means that something bad is about to happen, or a dead body is nearby."

—SEBASTIAN CROW

CHAPTER 1

This time, he wouldn't make the same mistake. He wouldn't stay quiet. There were no witnesses, but he knew he couldn't let that stop him. Sebastian Crow thought about all the years he waited, hoping for a different outcome, but knowing that what he did when he was a young father had set the tide for what was unfolding in front of him today.

Now, in his sixty-fifth year, he should be planning his retirement and shining up the custom-made Lund he had wanted to buy so he could spend hours fishing while anchored in Big Mouth Bay. Instead, he was trying to sort out the events of the last fifteen years and wondered how he didn't see any of this coming.

Sebastian turned his head and glanced behind him and he frantically scanned the street to see if he was being followed. Not that it mattered much, anyhow. Lake Pines was small, and everyone knew where he lived, especially since he owned the oldest plumbing business in town. Plus, he learned over the last several years that most of the town's residents went out of their way to avoid him. He turned around and refocused his gaze on the dock as he lumbered down the steep hill hoping not to fall, and desperately gasping for air as he ran.

Or as close to running that Sebastian Crow could manage.

"Damn it," Sebastian yelled as the thin plastic handle on the Food Mart bag snapped free of his swollen fingers. The bag fell to the ground and the milk carton exploded. A wave of milk splashed against his leg, soaking his pants. Three apples rolled out and sprayed milk in the air as they tumbled through the white puddle and bowled toward the water. He ignored the mess on the street and kicked aside both the bag and carton and continued toward the dock.

Moving as quickly as he could manage.

He regretted parking his boat at the far end of the Main Street dock as he struggled to make his way down the road that led to the water. The road sloped from its peak in the center of town and snaked a path toward the town's bay. Canadian Shield lined the shore and stretched out into the middle of Lake Pine's Bay just below the water's surface, forcing the town to build the boat slips in a narrow, extended design.

Lake Pines was a summer retreat for Sebastian's family ever since he was a child. When his mother would turn the calendar's page from April to May, Sebastian would begin the countdown to the long weekend when he would venture down to the lake with his father and prepare the camp and cottage for their family's summer holiday. That's when Sebastian learned the important skills that would guide him into his chosen profession.

Plumbing a cottage on an island required a blend of drainage system knowledge and pure creativity. Often having less than a foot of crawl space to work within, Sebastian would have to improvise with connections and joints that could hold the onslaught of flushes and drains that carried water and waste into the septic tank that sat in the low lying field next to their cottage.

He finally convinced his father to let him build a trap door on the hall floor that would make it easy for him to access the many pipe joints and spare him the awkward motion of belly crawls to reach the center of the building. Which was often needed after a leak had occurred and an emergency repair was required. The trap door came in handy many times when a plumbing disaster would arise or a late-night escape to (or return from) a cottage party was necessary.

It also became a trademark building modification in many of the cottages that Sebastian worked on. His services were in high demand because of the many renovations and customizations that were being made to century-old family cottages, but his size made it difficult to negotiate the tight spaces he often was forced to work around.

Sebastian never appreciated the many diets and health kicks that Isobella would challenge him to try. His wife, if he could call her that, was a strict vegetarian and part-time yoga instructor that ran their house like she ran her classes. She abhorred clutter, preferred silence, and always expected that everyone would do what she asked. With no questions asked. After a time, Isobella and Sebastian could no longer live in the same house while trying to avoid each other and finally decided to live apart.

Neither of them wanted a divorce, something each of them saw as a sign of weakness and failure. However, in hindsight, they both knew it would have been the smarter choice and would allow each of them to live their own separate lives for good. But filing for divorce would mean they needed to communicate and possibly see each other, and that was something that neither of them was prepared to do. Once they agreed to live apart, Isobella packed three bags, left their house, and moved to Vancouver to live with her sister. Sebastian packed the few items of clothing he needed and moved permanently out to his cottage, selling the house and contents and sending half the money to Isobella.

And they haven't spoken since that day.

Now Sebastian knew he couldn't avoid calling her. He didn't know how he was going to find her or even if she still lived in Vancouver but there was no way around him needing to make this call.

Sebastian pounded along the pavement and landed with a thud on the old planks of the dock. Each step sent an echo reverberating in the space below the planks. Waves swayed below the boards and splashed against the rocky shoal shoreline that the dock system was anchored to. Sprays of water soaked the boards and green moss formed where water regularly wet the wood. Sebastian spread his feet apart and bent his legs to steady his heavy body on the floating dock. With each step he took, the dock swayed with this weight and rocked left to right. Threatening to toss Sebastian into the water with each wobble.

Sebastian's doctor stopped weighing him during his annual visits when Sebastian made it clear he had no intention of changing his lifestyle.

"I'm going to eat what I like, drink what I like, and smoke what I like," he warned Doctor Foster, when the gentle intern suggested a milder lifestyle that could guide him into old age with fewer aches and pains. And for a while, Doctor Foster was one of the few residents of Lake Pines who would acknowledge Sebastian with a kind word. Except for when someone needed his desired plumbing expertise.

As he neared his boat, he defied gravity as he ran toward the ropes. With one swift yank, he released the knots that held his boat in place and catapulted his body into the hull of the vessel. He cranked the key, and without looking behind him, he pushed the throttle control shifter into reverse. Before he was out of the slip, he spun the wheel hard to the right, then quickly straightened it before slamming the throttle forward. Driving a boat was second nature to most people who spent their life on the water, much like walking was to others. Before he was fully clear of the slip, Sebastian slipped the gear out of reverse and lowered the throttle to full.

As the boat picked up speed, Sebastian's body lurched back into the seat. His hands nervously grasped the controls and ignoring the waves and warning buoys, he steered his boat through Lake Pines Bay and out of the channel.

The burning sun seared his forehead where the sweat beads coated his pale skin. He reached for his glasses that were perched on the top of his head and realized that he had lost them at some point during his run to his boat. Sebastian dragged the back of his hand across his forehead and wiped the sweat from his brow. His thinning white hair, now disheveled and matted to his head.

He squinted his eyes against the setting sun as he drove around the back of Turnbull Island and into the stretch of water where his island was protected from the rolling storms that would batter most cottages on this part of the lake.

His father petitioned the province for three consecutive summers to grant him the right to rename the island. When his father purchased the densely treed six-acre island, a provincial surveyor had named it White Birch Island. Sebastian's father argued that a nameless government worker shouldn't hold the final say in the property's name that he legally, and rightfully, owned. Whether it was Sebastian's father's success in debating his case or the government's exhaustion in dealing with him, the island was officially renamed Crow Island the summer Sebastian turned four.

The name of the island grew to hold two distinct meanings.

The first, being the most obvious since it was the surname of the owners of the property.

The second became more of a mystical folklore when a family of crows nested on the island and made it a breeding ground every summer, growing their numbers as each year passed.

When friends would ask Sebastian why a large number of crows would congregate around his cottage he would say, "Most ancient cultures believe that crows are an omen and can guide humans into the afterlife. Some believe the crow to be sacred and hold mystical powers. All I know is that when there is a murder of crows around you, you need to leave, because it either means that something bad is about to happen, or a dead body is nearby."

Those that knew Sebastian well would laugh when he would utter the saying, but those who weren't as familiar with his sense of humor, would feel a chill run up their spine.

The sun was setting further down into the horizon as he neared the island, and it had now fallen below the treeline, no longer blinding his vision of the boathouse. Sebastian slowed the boat as he approached the slip and cut the engine as the tip of the boat entered the boathouse. He thrust out his large hand and grabbed hold of the dock cleat and yanked the boat to a stop. With the back rope in one hand, he stepped up on the back seat and hoisted his achy body onto the dock. He wrapped the single rope around the cleat and figured that would have to do for now. He'd deal with the boat later.

Sebastian struggled as he climbed the ten wooden steps to the cottage lawn. His breathing was heavy, and he was getting lightheaded with the exertion that he rarely put his body through.

Pine cones and dried evergreen needles carpeted the ground and concealed the sunken stone path that led to the cottage. Each of Sebastian's steps upon the fallen debris echoed a crunch under the weight of his tattered shoes. He long since stopped sweeping them clear. He preferred their scent to a clean path and since he had lived here alone since the day Isobella left, there was no one around who could complain about them.

He wouldn't even be able to guess how old the trees were that surrounded the cottage. They were fully grown and towered over the roof of the cottage ever since he could remember. Sebastian's father cleared the birch forest below the enormous jack pines when he bought the island, knowing it would be the perfect location for their cottage. Even against the builder's advice, who warned that he would regret building a cottage that close to so many enormous trees. Pollen and pine needles coated the roof, and depending on the light and time of year, it would either appear to be a deep green or a reddish-brown, disguising the true color of the shingles.

The brown paint on the thin strips of siding had long since faded, and the stone steps were chipped at the base. Oversized trees reluctantly surrendered their heavy branches to a violent storm that rolled over the island three summers earlier. In its wake, several of the second-floor windows were left broken and shattered. Sebastian had boarded closed most of the windows instead of replacing the shattered panes of glass. He rarely spent time on the second floor, a combined result of his weak knees and painful memories. Maintenance was made more difficult over the last five years for Sebastian with his faltering health as well as his increasing girth. Climbing a ladder was impossible and kneeling on the ground to apply cement patches on the stone would require him to be able to stand up when he was done. And he was sure he couldn't do that alone.

Instead, Sebastian decided to fade into the final season of his life at the same pace that the cottage did. It somehow, he thought, seemed appropriate.

Sebastian stepped onto the creaking porch and grabbed hold of the spindled railing, hoisting his body up the two steps that in his youth he would easily leap over. He pulled on the screen door when he reached the front of the cottage at the far end of the porch. Moths had begun to gather at the top of the frame with the late day's warmth and flew toward his face when he swung the door open. He waved them away with this right hand as he thrust his body into the cottage. He slammed the interior door closed, and for the first time in decades he bolted the two thick brass locks on the wooden door and lowered the blinds.

He moved along each windowsill and flipped every latch closed, pushing each one to ensure they would hold closed. When the door at the back of the cottage was finally secured, Sebastian let out a deep sigh of relief.

He stood in the center of the living room and forced his breathing to a steady pace and dried the final dampness from his brow with the collar of his t-shirt and ran his fingers through his thinning white hair.

He glanced around the room and wondered how things turned out so different than how he had planned. He reminisced about the day when he was standing in this very room when his father handed him the deed to the cottage along with the responsibility of the family name into Sebastian's keeping. There was so much promise when he started out. At first, Isobella was as eager as he was to build a life together and to give their children the gift that Sebastian had while growing up.

This cottage, they promised each other, would be what anchored their family together.

Sebastian shook those memories from his head and walked over to the glass cabinet at the far end of the room. He turned the small iron key and released the lock on the glass door of the antique cabinet that held his favorite whiskey bottle and the short crystal glasses he and his father would drink from.

The first glass warmed his throat and calmed his mind. He took his time with the second glass and sipped it slowly as he looked out the front window and watched the bay where the boathouse sat.

The waves rolled in, pushed by the evening wind and creating small whitecaps as they neared the shallow shore. Shadows from the island's trees cascaded across the bay and darkened the water around the island.

A chill ran over Sebastian, seeping into his skin now coarse with goosebumps.

Darkness would come quickly tonight, and Sebastian hoped he could sleep after what happened earlier in town.

He decided to wait until morning before he would track down Isobella and call her. He wanted to figure out exactly how he was going to tell her. What was he going to say?

Sebastian drained the last of the whiskey from his glass and leaned back in the faded wicker chair which protested his girth with a squeak.

He closed his eyes.

At first, Sebastian thought the clicking sound was the noise from the branches knocking against the roof, being pushed there by the wind. But when Sebastian heard the familiar creaking sound of the aged and rusted hinges on the trap door in the hall floor, he knew that two whiskeys wouldn't be enough to help him through what was going to happen next.

Sebastian turned toward the creaking sound in the hall and waited. Heavy boots echoed footsteps from the hall as the intruder approached the front room where Sebastian waited. And outside, a murder of crows gathered on the jack pines that hovered over the cottage and they cawed, echoing their warning.

Sebastian saw no other choice but to laugh at the premonition he so often made in jest but was now threatening to come true.

CHAPTER 2

It was the first of July and instead of floating in her boat in Lake Pines Bay with Simon waiting for the fireworks to begin, Kerry was on her way to help secure a crime scene for a murder investigation at a local cottage. The last murder investigation she was involved with took place the preceding December, and Kerry would have been happy if she hadn't had another like that ever again.

It wasn't the crime scene that disturbed her. She was, after all, a trained coroner and was used to seeing dismembered and disfigured corpses.

It was the trauma of dealing with distraught family members who wanted answers quickly that was the emotionally draining part. Especially after a local reporter approached the family before the police told them that someone close to them had been murdered.

"Thanks for coming out on such short notice Doctor Dearborne," Wayne Burgess still was unaccustomed to calling Kerry by her first name and she had learned to live with it.

Most of the time.

In fact, she often had fun and teased him about it and would call him by his official title now and again, "It's alright Constable Burgess. It's my job."

Wayne nodded, but kept his face turned forward as he steered the police boat through the channel that led them to the far side of Turnbull Island.

"How d'you like your gift?" Wayne asked, changing the subject.

"Let's say it was a bit of a surprise," Kerry said, not wanting to reveal her true feelings about Simon's choice of a birthday gift this year. In fact, she wasn't really sure how she felt about it.

"What are you going to name it?" Wayne asked.

"Not sure," Kerry's idea of a birthday gift had not included four paws a tail, and a regular bathroom routine, but somehow Simon thought it was what she needed.

Wayne raised his arm and pointed to an island that was positioned at the far end of the bay, "Crow Island is just ahead. It's the one with the large boathouse."

Kerry peered over the front window of the boat and saw two boats that were already tied to the front dock and a haze shone from beneath the tree cover on the island from the portable spotlights that were set up on the lawn next to the cottage.

"Who found the victim?" Kerry asked.

"One of his employees," Wayne said. "His name is Paul Barrett. We sent him home after an officer took his statement. He was pretty shaken up over seeing the victim so badly beaten. The victim didn't show up on a job site this morning and after trying to reach him all morning, he drove out to see if he was okay. He was sixty-five."

Kerry shook her head at the inference that anyone the age of sixty-five should warrant any additional concern over someone of a younger age. Her father was sixty-five and was still running a mile every morning. If she couldn't get in touch with him one morning, she would have assumed he was out for a longer run or having a coffee with any of the multitudes of friends he kept in contact with. But then again, not everyone was like her father.

"Who's at the scene right now?" Kerry had learned to try and not sound so possessive over crime or accident scenes where she was working, but it was hard to deal with incompetent staff who felt that they were living a real-life version of a television cop show. Someone would inadvertently touch a crucial piece of evidence or move something to cover the body thinking that they

16

were giving the victim some respect, but in fact, they were making it harder to solve the case and secure crucial evidence.

"I sent Sally, Greg, and Aidan out ahead to secure the scene," Wayne said.

Kerry felt better knowing that they were there. Greg and Sally were too new to take control of the crime scene, and Aidan had years of experience and enough leadership qualities that he could take responsibility for the entire investigation if he had to.

"Good," Kerry said, pleased with Wayne's choices.

Wayne smacked his forehead with the palm of his hand, "Shoot, I didn't even think of asking Simon to come along. Sorry."

Kerry waved Wayne's apology off, "That's okay. Not exactly the best date night environment."

Simon had just graduated from the academy and was interning with the police department in Lake Pines. He and Wayne worked remarkably well together considering they had been close friends their whole life. Simon had no problem taking commanding orders from Wayne and Wayne didn't see it as a power trip in having Simon as his subordinate. Even though anyone in the department could see that Simon was more suited to be a commanding officer than Wayne was.

"Weren't you both going to watch the fireworks tonight?" Wayne asked.

Kerry nodded, "Yep. We've been doing that every Canada Day since we met. He's out there now. I told him not to wait for me since we will probably be more than a few hours."

Wayne let out a sigh and nodded. He wasn't the most patient of police officers, but Kerry knew she'd be able to keep him focused for the evening if she gave him enough minor tasks to run.

Wayne pulled up to the end of the dock and parked perpendicular to the two boats that were already moored along the side. Kerry grabbed the ladder and hoisted her body up onto the dock while holding onto her bag. Wayne tossed her the back rope and she tied it to the cleat as he climbed out from the bow with the front rope and secured the front of the boat to the ladder.

Crow Island was heavily treed, and it was difficult to get an unobstructed view of the cottage from the dock. However, the closer they walked to it, Kerry could see that it was once a simple but clean cottage. The rooflines and the large windows would have provided an unrestricted view of the bay and the rising sun in the morning.

"What happened to this place?" Kerry asked as she surveyed the dilapidated state of the building and the surrounding property.

The stairs that led from the dock to the cottage leaned to one side and the once dark brown stain was eroded in the center where years of steps tread over them. The railings were cracked, splintered, and faded from weather and wear. Pine cones, branches, and decomposing leaves littered the edges of the steps and Kerry could smell the decay and moss that formed on the frame of the stairs and under the brush.

"Good evening Doctor Dearborne," Sally greeted them with a nod. "Good evening Constable Burgess."

"Good evening Sally," Wayne said. "Is everything secured inside?"

"Yes sir," Sally said. "We were just waiting for you to arrive before we did anything else."

"Have you started taking pictures of the crime scene yet?" Kerry asked.

"Yes, Doctor Dearborne. Aidan, err uh, Officer Green had Greg and I take them before we lost the light," Sally said.

Kerry smiled, "Good. Why don't we go inside?"

Kerry pulled a pair of gloves out of her pocket and when she noticed Wayne patting his pockets down in search of his, she handed her gloves to him, "Here, I have an extra pair."

"Thanks," Wayne mumbled apologetically as he took the gloves.

Kerry pulled another pair from her pocket and snapped them over her hands.

She glanced around the side of the cottage and noticed it looked very much like the front yard did. A thick carpet of pine cones blanketed the ground. Years of trees shedding needles, pine cones, branches, and leaves piled over the ground making it impossible for a lawn to grow in the area. Small patches of sparse strings of grass blades shot up from the rot to reveal that at one time a lush lawn may have surrounded the cottage.

The entrance to the cottage was made even darker from the thickness of the evergreens that draped over the roof. As she walked closer to the building Kerry realized the darkened branches were not because of the thick growth of dense branches but a mass congregation of birds that huddled at the top of the trees.

Crows silently lined the branches and lingered above the forensic team that worked under the artificial light, coming and going from the cottage at various stages of the evening. Kerry felt a chill run up her spine as she watched a few crows lift from the branches of the trees and regain their perch atop the roof. Almost as if they were lying in wait.

Kerry turned her attention to the ground and made a mental note to search the area when there was daylight for traces of footsteps or a path that the killer may have taken as they made their way into the cottage to where the victim was attacked. But for tonight they'd keep their investigation to the interior of the building.

Kerry opened the door and walked directly into the crime scene, careful to step over the broken glass from the door.

On the floor lay a man that looked much older than his apparent sixty-five years. His five-foot-ten frame was easily over two hundred pounds and was stretched out in a darkened pool of blood.

Except for the bloodied body covered in stab wounds, the room appeared to be untouched. Years of dust lay undisturbed, piles of faded magazines with curled up edges were perched against the fireplace hearth waiting to be used to start a fire and a glass with sticky remnants of an amber liquor was placed on a small white table next to an oversized wicker chair turned facing toward the front window and out over the bay.

A stack of board games was nestled in the corner pleading to be played but looked like they hadn't been touched in decades. Colored boxes of Clue, Masterpiece, and Monopoly all faded with a thick layer of dust that accumulated over their cardboard surfaces.

Nothing was overturned, out of place, or disturbed.

"The victim didn't seem to give up much of a struggle," Kerry said aloud.

"He was old," Wayne alleged, as a reason for his submission to a knife-wielding murderer.

Kerry turned to face him, "Wayne, I don't care if you are Mr. Barrington, if someone is coming at you with a knife that many times, there is going to be some amount of a struggle."

Mr. Barrington was Lake Pines' oldest citizen and primary celebrity. He had turned ninety-eight in June and the town threw him a parade for his birthday and his only reply was, "*I would have been happy with a cake.*" He was unofficially Lake Pines example of how to age gracefully and with the right attitude.

Kerry found a clear spot on the floor and placed her bag down. She checked the body for any signs of a struggle or trauma that wasn't related to the obvious stab wounds on the body.

Wayne spoke, knowing what Kerry was thinking at that moment, and answered her question before she asked it, "His name is Sebastian Crow. He lived here alone for as long as I can remember, and he owns Crow

Plumbing and has worked on cottages and homes in the area since he moved here when he was twenty-four."

"No family?" Kerry asked as she walked around the body.

"None that I know of," Wayne said.

"I think he had a wife, but she left some time ago," Sally said as she looked on. "At least that's what I've heard."

"Kids?" Kerry asked, not lifting her gaze from the victim's body.

"Not sure," Sally said. "Rumor has it that they ran away."

"Any factual information?" Kerry asked.

Sally blushed, realizing she may have overstepped her boundaries as a new hire.

Kerry lifted her head and let a sympathetic smile cross her face, "Just find out for sure. Okay?"

Sally nodded.

Kerry stood and looked around the room.

"Did you dust the door for prints?" Kerry said as she pointed to the broken glass on the floor and the cracked door.

"That was broken by Paul, his employee who came to check on him. He panicked when he saw Sebastian laying on the floor covered in blood. He just tried to get in quickly and since the door was locked, he had to break it down," Wayne said.

"What about the other doors?" Kerry asked.

"I had the officers dust for prints on those, but we probably won't get anything," Wayne said.

"Why's that?" Kerry asked.

"All the doors were locked from the inside. Windows too. They were all bolted tight."

"I find it hard to believe that Mr. Crow could have been attacked so brutally and there not be a trace of that anywhere in this cottage. Keep looking," Kerry instructed the three officers who stood behind Wayne, attentively listening to each word.

The three officers scurried off in separate directions in search of any evidence that the killer may have left behind.

Wayne stepped a little closer to Kerry and the body, "So, what do you think?"

"What do you think?" Kerry asked in response.

"I think it is obviously a robbery gone wrong," Wayne said as he folded his arms across his chest.

Kerry stretched her arms out and waved them around the room, "Of what?"

Wayne crumpled his brows and looked at Kerry but didn't have an answer.

"Nothing is overturned, there is not even one scratch on the victim as if he was trying to defend his home. There are no apparent marks on his fingers and both his arms are stretched out from his body with no bruising or scratches on his forearms," Kerry then pointed to the glass on the table. "This is a man who was enjoying an evening drink while looking out at his property. One that is so aptly named after him and that he has owned for quite some time. Even in this ramshackle state, would you not have put up some degree of a fight if you were being robbed?"

Wayne looked at the room, trinkets untouched, paintings still hanging on the wall and his watch still strapped around his wrist.

"I guess."

Kerry stared at the face of the man that lay on the floor in front of her and who seemed to be silently pleading with her for answers.

"There's something we're missing, and we need to find it if we are going to track down Mr. Crow's killer."

Kerry knelt beside the body and snapped open the clasp on her bag and pulled out her coroner's thermometer. She slid it out of its protective cover and lifted the victim's shirt.

"Oh god, I hate this part," Wayne covered his mouth and turned around.

Kerry positioned the stainless-steel probe above the victim's midsection and gently pushed down, "We need to determine the time of death Wayne. Don't worry, I'll keep the worst of it in my lab."

Kerry read the temperature and recorded it in her logbook and then slowly removed the thermometer and wiped it clean.

"Doctor Dearborne, Constable Burgess. You're going to want to see this," Aidan hurriedly escorted them from the room and into the back hall.

On the edge of an antique cabinet, the faint impression of a partial bloody mark was visible. It had dried to a dark shade and could easily have been missed against the dark mahogany wood.

"Is there enough to lift a fingerprint from?" Kerry asked.

"It doesn't look like it, but we'll give it a try," the young officer said.

Kerry returned to the victim and continued her initial examination of the body and the surrounding crime scene. Once she was satisfied that there was nothing else to record, she instructed the team to prepare the body for transport back to her lab. With few indications of a struggle and numerous stab wounds, Kerry recognized the hallmark signs in this crime scene.

Without knowing what happened or who the killer was, one thing was for certain. This murder was personal, and that meant it was going to get messy.

CHAPTER 3

Kerry had missed the fireworks and by the time she had made sure the victim's body was safely, and properly, transported to her lab it was past midnight. Kerry pulled her Jeep alongside Simon's truck in the driveway and put it in park. She had a feeling that he would be waiting up for her, which he usually did on the nights she worked late.

When she turned the corner at the end of the street, the front of their lawn was illuminated with the yellow light that cascaded from the front porch lamp glowing above the door. She was only on the first step when the front door unlocked, and Simon held it open for her. He yawned as she stepped inside, the new unnamed puppy at his feet.

"How were the fireworks?" Kerry asked.

"Okay. Not as good without you," Simon kissed Kerry and closed the door. "I took the boys with me, and they loved it. And Karen was happy to get them off her hands for a few hours."

"Those nephews of yours are pretty lucky to have you as an uncle," Kerry hugged him.

"So, how was Crow Island?" Simon asked.

"It's going to be a messy investigation," Kerry said. "Is there any way I can convince you to tag along with Wayne on this one?"

"Sure," Simon said. "Any particular reason?"

"I just want to make sure he doesn't rush this one along. There are too many missing pieces right now," Kerry explained. "I'll know more tomorrow."

"Then we should get some rest," Simon locked the door and turned off the light.

Together they walked upstairs and got ready for bed.

Within ten minutes of crawling under the covers, Simon was in a deep sleep and the puppy was nestled between them in the gully created by the down comforter.

However, sleep didn't come as easily for Kerry and her mind eventually wandered to what she saw on Crow Island and the murder of crows that gathered outside the cottage.

* * *

Kerry arrived at her lab at eight-thirty the next morning eager to make sense of Sebastian Crow's murder and to hopefully find a solid clue that would point them toward the killer. Earlier in the year, she was able to convince Peter to give her the funding so she could hire a summer student. She wanted to prove that not only did Lake Pines need a second set of hands in the coroner's office, but that she could also help with the necessary training of the next generation of pathologists.

Constable Peter George had been promoted to Sergeant Peter George in the middle of last winter after he broke up a drug ring that was distressing the residents in the small towns in the area for several years. In addition to frightening the residents, their presence also significantly brought down property values and kept new businesses from opening. There wasn't only a push from the residents to clean up the streets but from the government who was worried the towns could suffer to a point of no return.

With Peter having been promoted it also selfishly benefited Kerry. She had a strong working relationship with him and was happy to find out he was also going to oversee all her funding. Kerry wasted no time in petitioning him for an intern and was thrilled when he approved her request.

Within days of the funding approval, Kerry hired Sophia Della Cruz. She and her family had recently immigrated from the Philippines and she had a difficult time finding work, along with her own identity, in the small town of Lake Pines. Kerry had met Sophia's family when she was volunteering with the new residents' committee and was the one who approached Sophia and suggested she apply for the job, which included fully paid training along with the position. Because of that, she didn't have to worry about her lack of experience and since Kerry knew Sophia was very bright, she wouldn't have trouble with the scientific nature of the job either. Kerry's intuition was right, and Sophia took to the job quickly and showed great promise in a very short period of time.

If Kerry's intuition was right, this murder case was going to give Sophia a dose of much-needed experience. The kind she could never get in a classroom.

After she and Sophia placed the body on the examining table Kerry got to work assessing the body in more depth. She filled Sophia in along the way on what she knew about the victim, which wasn't much.

"We're working with very little information here Doctor Dearborne," Sophia said as she pushed the medical tray next to where Kerry was standing.

"There's more information here than it seems Sophia," Kerry said. "Just because there isn't a suspect yet doesn't mean that we can't figure out *who* killed

Sebastian Crow. The first step is to figure out *what* killed Sebastian Crow."

Accentuating the words *who* and *what.*

Sophia glanced at the bare body, now cleaned and prepped for examination, and counted seven stab wounds on his torso, "It looks like he was stabbed to death."

"That would be a standard presumption considering he had been stabbed seven times, however," Kerry walked over to the victim's right arm and lifted it in the air, turning it slightly to reveal the underside of his forearm. "The victim was right-handed. So why wouldn't he have had at least some scratches or defensive marks on his arm?"

"Was he wearing a thick shirt?" Sophia asked.

"No. He was wearing a cotton t-shirt when he was killed. His arms were bare," Kerry explained.

"Then he was stabbed *after* he was killed," Sophia said.

"Exactly," Kerry agreed. "Now we just need to figure out what killed him first."

"Do you want me to run a sample of what was in the victim's glass? Maybe he was poisoned," Sophia asked.

"Let's run it to be sure, but I don't think that would be the reason judging by where the body was found," Kerry said. "Constable Burgess should be getting the results for the bloody fingerprint that was left at the scene later today."

Sophia excused herself from the examination room and went to the lab in the next room and began to swab the glass for testing. Although she was sure that there were no signs of a struggle, Kerry examined Sebastian's hands and skin under a microscope to be certain.

Sebastian Crow wasn't a healthy man and the autopsy of his organs was sure to confirm that, however, there was no doubt that his hands and arms held the strength necessary to at least try and defend himself in the event of an attack. Especially one that threatened his life.

Kerry ran her fingers over the back of Sebastian's head and then along his spine. There were no anomalies in his skull or spine. So, she could rule out Sebastian having been hit over the head and knocked to the ground.

As she moved her hand from the back of his neck to the front, Kerry's fingers sensed a kink in an artery at the side of his neck. Sebastian's girth and thickness prevented the normal visual inspection to catch it at the scene.

There was only one other time that Kerry saw an injury like that which was a cause of death. A thirty-eight-year-old man was found dead with no apparent sign of trauma. His wife returned home to find him on the floor of their living room. He hadn't been beaten, there was no robbery and he wasn't bleeding. Initially, the cause of death was recorded as a massive stroke but as the coroner examined the body further, he discovered that his neck had been manipulated thereby severing an artery. Eventually, his friend admitted to trying to adjust the victim's neck the same way his chiropractor does, but when he twisted his friend's head, he just fell still. The incident was ruled an accidental death, but the case had been used many times in the training of young coroners.

Kerry reached for her scalpel and ran it along the side of Sebastian's neck and peeled back a layer of skin. She folded down the arm on her microscope and examined the artery. Sure enough, it had been severed at the base where it ran under his collarbone.

Now that she was certain what caused Sebastian Crow's death, she needed to figure out what was used to stab him with post-mortem.

No bloody weapon was found at the scene and knowing what object to look for could prove useful when narrowing down who the killer could be. There was one thing the courts loved and that was solid physical evidence.

The shape and the length of the stab wounds weren't like those that were associated with a standard kitchen knife. The edges of the wounds were frayed and extended deep into the body. Judging by the angle and the depth of the wounds, Kerry speculated Sebastian was already laying on the floor when he was stabbed repeatedly by his killer. The weapon, although, was a little more difficult to describe. Kerry completed the autopsy and then cleaned and sutured the body. Normally she'd be preparing the body to be transported to the Lake Pines Mortuary where the family was waiting to plan their funeral service. As far as Wayne knew Sebastian Crow lived alone and had no family to speak of.

Finding a family member or someone who was close to Sebastian Crow may also help in determining if he had any enemies. Sebastian Crow wasn't the victim of a robbery gone wrong.

He was stabbed seven times after he was dead, and with great force. This was a crime of passion. There was something personal about the murder of Sebastian Crow and Kerry wanted to find out what it was.

Where were the answers?

Kerry instinctively knew they lay with the non-existent family and the lone bloody fingerprint that they couldn't trace.

CHAPTER 4

Sebastian Crow's financial records were a surprise and shock to Kerry as Wayne spread them across his desk. The dilapidated state of his cottage and his old scratched boat led Kerry to believe he was barely getting by. In fact, Sebastian was a very wealthy man. His plumbing business had been a success since the day he started working in the Lake Pines area in his mid-twenties. With few bills and a steady stream of cash flow, Sebastian was able to save a large amount of money over the years.

"Do you think someone was blackmailing him?" Kerry asked. "He did have a lot of money."

Wayne shrugged his shoulders, "It's possible, but not likely. Sebastian was more of a recluse and most people we spoke with just thought he was an odd old man. He had no complaints from his customers, but none would say they liked him either. His business had an A1 rating with the Better Business Bureau and there were never any complaints filed against his business. I had Simon canvas the main businesses in town and ask around to see if anyone knew Sebastian Crow or had any dealings with him. Except for the Food Mart on Second Avenue, not many people had contact with him. Simon even got the impression that maybe Sebastian Crow wasn't well-liked, but no one would go into any specific detail."

"So, no one knows anything about him?" Kerry asked.

"I didn't say that," Wayne said with a smirk. "He apparently was in a protracted legal battle with his neighbor."

"I thought Sebastian Crow was the only one living on that island?"

"He was. It was the owner of the island next to his," Wayne lifted a sheet of paper from his desk and read the name. "Tom Pruitt is his name. You won't believe what he is suing our deceased Mr. Crow about."

"I'm sure I would have no idea," Kerry hated the guessing games Wayne played.

"His crows!" Wayne laughed.

"What!"

"Sebastian took to the corvids quite easily. Having grown up with them and all, and even had a few as a pet. He always made sure they had ample sources of food and eventually they learned that Crow Island was a safe haven for them, and they nested there in huge numbers. Although, not because of the name of course." Wayne explained.

"Of course," Kerry said, finding it difficult not to smile. "Is Tom Pruitt someone we may want to speak with?"

"I would say so. He was overheard threatening Sebastian as they were leaving court last week," Wayne said.

"What kind of threat?" Kerry asked.

"The court guard reported he heard Mr. Pruitt say, 'those birds won't be a problem once you're gone' or something along those lines," Wayne said, reading from the report.

"I'd say that *is* a threat that could be considered passionate. When can you speak with him?" Kerry asked eager to find the person who killed Sebastian Crow.

"I have an officer picking him up right now. We can speak with him as soon as he gets here," Wayne said.

"Okay, good. You said Sebastian Crow started his business when he was in his mid-twenties. He couldn't have always kept to himself," Kerry said.

"You're right," Wayne waved Sally over to his desk. The young officer hurried over to where he and Kerry were talking.

"Yes sir," Sally said.

"Were you able to find anything out about Mr. Crow?" Wayne asked.

Sally nodded and handed Wayne three printouts from her computer. Kerry could see that her report was neatly typed and organized. Maybe there was some promise for this young officer yet.

Wayne's eyebrows revealed surprise as he read the report that Sally compiled. He handed the first two sheets to Kerry while he finished reading the last one.

Kerry quickly glanced at the sheet and the highlighted items, "He was married?"

"*Is* married," Wayne corrected Kerry. "He and Isobella never got divorced. She left Lake Pines fifteen years ago, the same time he sold his house in town and moved to the island."

"We need to track down Isobella Crow," Kerry said. "She could have some insight as to who may have wanted Sebastian dead."

"I'm on it," Sally said. "I ran a trace on Isobella Crow. She moved to Vancouver after she left Lake Pines and now lives up near Whistler. She runs a yoga retreat in Squamish. I have her contact information." Sally handed a sheet with Isobella's phone number and address.

"Great job Sally," Wayne said. "I will call her now. Someone needs to claim the body, it may as well be his wife."

"But they haven't been together for fifteen years," Kerry said. "Isn't it going to be weird for her to come down and deal with Sebastian's death?"

"I'm sure it will be, but legally she is his wife, and look," Wayne handed Kerry the last sheet he was holding in his hands. "This is the list of properties Sebastian owned at the time of his death. He never changed the title of ownership for Crow Island. Isobella is listed as the joint owner. The island is hers now."

"There's something else sir," Sally interrupted.

"Yes," Wayne said.

"He and Isobella had two kids together. A boy and a girl." Sally added.

"Any idea where they are now?" Kerry asked.

Sally shook her head, "School records show that Katrina, their daughter, moved to Toronto and went to Humber College. She graduated from their nursing program a few years later."

"And the boy?" Kerry asked.

"His name is Kyle. He ran away when he was sixteen and I don't think he ever came back. I don't think he would have wanted to either," Sally said.

"Why is that?" Kerry asked.

"There was a report filed by his school with child services. Kyle's gym teacher had noticed several bruises and a few questionable marks on his back and arms that made him suspicious," Sally explained.

"If he was an active teen it wouldn't have been uncommon," Kerry explained. "I have seen some parents wrongly accused just because of some misinterpreted bruising."

"It wasn't just the bruises. His gym teacher said they looked more like burns. That, and the fact that he was acting out a lot and starting fights all the time," Sally twisted her mouth. "It's sad to think he felt he had to leave just to feel safe."

"I agree," Kerry suddenly had a sinister impression of her victim who lived alone on Crow Island. At first, she thought it was sad that Sebastian Crow lived alone, now she thought he may have deserved it. The enigmatic victim was quickly becoming unlikable. "Were you able to locate either of his kids?"

"Just the daughter. I added her contact information underneath Isobella's number," Sally explained as she pointed to the sheet of paper in Wayne's hand.

"Let's start with the wife," Wayne said. "It'll be somewhat easier to tell an estranged spouse her husband has been murdered than it will be to tell his child."

Sally returned to her desk to continue to search for any trace of Kyle, but Kerry knew that if he left at such a young age that he could easily have slipped into several bad situations. A chill ran up Kerry's spine when she thought of all the innocent victims who were put in further danger just trying to avoid an abusive situation at home, and she wondered if that's what happened to Kyle.

Wayne sat down and pulled his phone to the middle of his desk and he began to dial the number that was listed for Isobella's yoga retreat. Kerry could hear the echo of the rings from where she sat across from Wayne's desk.

"Hello," Isobella's voice was sharp and rang through the headset that was pressed against Wayne's ear.

"Hello, is this Isobella Crow?" Wayne asked.

"It's Isobella Frank, but yes I was Isobella Crow. What can I do for you?" Isobella asked with a distrustful tone in her voice. "If Sebastian owes you any money you can forget about getting it from me, I haven't seen him in almost fifteen years."

"That's not what I'm calling about Ms. Frank," Wayne said. "I'm calling to inform you that Sebastian Crow has been murdered, and as you are still legally listed as his wife it's my obligation to notify you."

Silence occupied the next few minutes of the phone call.

"Oh, well, I didn't know," Isobella stammered. "Who did you say you were?"

"Constable Burgess at the Lake Pines police station. I'm here with Doctor Dearborne who is helping conduct the investigation into the death of your husband."

"Husband. Wow, that's weird to hear again," Isobella's voice had softened with the news of Sebastian's death. "Well, thank you for taking the time to notify me, but I really don't have anything to do with Sebastian anymore."

"I understand this is awkward Ms. Frank, but," Wayne was interrupted by Isobella who insisted he call her by her first name.

"Alright, Isobella," Wayne continued. "I know this is awkward, however, we are going to need someone to officially identify and claim the body. And since you are still listed as the joint owner for Crow Island, I figured you would have to come to town to settle the estate in any case."

"Sebastian never took my name off the deed?" Isobella asked.

"Apparently, not," Wayne said.

"Then I guess I'm going to need to make a trip to Lake Pines to settle things. For good, this time," Isobella said.

"We haven't contacted Katrina yet, would you like to call her?" Wayne asked.

"I haven't talked to her since she left Lake Pines. I wouldn't even know how to reach her. And Kyle, well, once he had a chance, he took off as fast as he could and we haven't seen him since," Isobella explained. "I left a few months after Kyle ran away. There was no point in sticking around with both kids gone."

"Would you like Katrina's number?" Wayne asked, slightly uncomfortable.

Isobella paused before she answered, "It may be better if you contact her directly. I'll let you know when I arrive in town."

Wayne gave Isobella his phone number and promised to have Sebastian's lawyer contact her when she arrived.

The call to Katrina was more representative of a child who lost her father. She broke down in tears and disbelief at the idea that her father had been murdered. Although Katrina had never returned to Lake Pines, she had been in contact with her father throughout the years. They shared phone calls on special occasions and kept up to date with each other's lives. When Wayne asked why she had never returned, Katrina said it was just too painful with everything that happened to their family.

Kerry could understand that. Sometimes it was easier to forgive when you didn't have to be face to face with the reminder of what hurt you in the first place. Kerry learned to not judge how others chose to deal with their pain. Not everyone needed to be in an episode of Dr. Phil for their wounds to be healed. She learned that herself, choosing to not revisit her painful past.

Katrina agreed to come to Lake Pines. She wanted to make sure her father had a respectful burial and she wasn't convinced her mother would do that. Wayne gave his number to Katrina and once he hung up, he returned his focus on the conversation with Kerry.

"I just checked with Sally and there's still no trace of Kyle," Kerry said. "He just seems to have dropped off the map."

"It's not uncommon for kids from small towns Kerry," Wayne explained. "I wouldn't even be surprised if he moved away and changed his name in order to start a new life. It happens more than you realize."

Wayne's phone rang and he reached out and picked up on the first ring, "Hello, Constable Burgess."

He nodded and thanked the caller and then lowered the phone.

"Tom Pruitt is here for questioning," Wayne informed Kerry as he walked around his desk. "This should be interesting."

Kerry followed him out of the room, "Why is that?"

"When my officer went to speak with him, he tried to run away," Wayne explained.

"That's odd if he doesn't have anything to hide," Kerry said. "Don't you think?"

"And there's something else," Wayne held the hall door open that led to the interrogation room and Kerry walked through. "He had a fresh gash across his forearm."

"Let me guess, from a large knife?" Kerry asked.

CHAPTER 5

Tom Pruitt was what most people would describe as a wily individual and his appearance aptly resonated with that description. He had a thin face, a pointed nose, and his small dark eyes (that were just a little too close together) darted around the room as he tried to make some sense of his situation.

Tufts of black hair poked through the trucker's cap he wore high on his head and piercings of a three-day-old beard covered his neck and face. He nervously shook his leg and drummed his right hand on the top of the table. His left arm had been cuffed to the table's leg and his face was streaked with dirt.

"You can't keep me here, I didn't do nothing wrong!" Tom snapped at Wayne as he and Kerry walked into the room.

"Well, my officer has a bruise on his cheek that says otherwise," Wayne pulled out a chair and sat directly across from Tom.

"He pushed me to the ground. What was I going to do?" Tom asked, his voice shaking and his cheeks growing red.

"How about coming in quietly to answer a few questions?" Wayne suggested. "Unless you have something to hide Mr. Pruitt."

Tom shot his attention to Kerry who sat down in the chair next to Wayne, "What's she doing here?"

"Doctor Dearborne is helping me with the investigation," Wayne explained. "And you're to give her the same cooperation as I expect you to give me."

Tom huffed and mumbled something indistinguishable under his breath.

"Why don't you start by explaining why you ran from Officer Grady today?" Wayne asked.

Tom shrugged his shoulders, "Do I need a lawyer?"

"Depends Tom, on what you did," Wayne leaned forward with his forearms on the table and folded his fingers together.

"I told you, I didn't do nothing!" Tom snapped and then pulled his left arm. "Do you need to cuff me like this?"

"As long as I think you want to slug one of us, yeah, we do," Wayne said.

"Am I being arrested?" Tom asked.

"I can arrest you for hitting Officer Grady as well as resisting arrest, but I really just wanted to ask you a couple of questions," Wayne explained.

Tom let out a frustrated huff, "About what?" he snapped.

"Your disagreement with Sebastian Crow."

"That crazy old man! He and his stupid crows. They keep me up all night, crap all over my house and they have ruined my gardens," Tom explained.

Kerry found it hard to believe that Tom Pruitt had a garden worth saving.

"And that's why you were suing him, right?" Kerry asked.

"Yeah. It's going to take a lot of money to repaint my place. And, those crazy birds go after my dog too!" Tom shook his head. "Sebastian is a crazy old man."

"So, it's safe to say there was bad blood between you two," Wayne said.

"Yeah, there was," Tom groaned. "Is that why I'm here?"

Wayne ignored Tom's question, "A court guard overheard you threaten Sebastian Crow when you were leaving court last week."

"I didn't threaten him," Tom snapped.

Wayne lifted a sheet from the table and read from his notes, "You said, and I quote, *'those birds won't be a problem once you're gone'.* You did say that, didn't you Tom?" Wayne asked.

"That's not a threat. *'I'll kill you'* is a threat," Tom said with a laugh.

"Did you want to?" Wayne asked.

"Want to what?"

"Kill Sebastian."

"It was just something I said, I didn't mean anything by it. I just want him to get rid of those crows. It's not normal to have those creepy birds hanging around anyway," Tom said.

"Like when you threatened Sam Southport five years ago?" Wayne pulled out the printout of a charge that was laid against Tom Pruitt when he lashed out at his supervisor at his job at the mill. Wayne slid it across the table to where Tom could read it.

"That was blown out of proportion," Tom explained. "That assho.."

"Hey!" Wayne interrupted Tom. "Language."

"That *jerk* refused to put me up for a promotion that was rightfully mine," Tom tried to explain. "Instead he gave it to that kid from Thunder Bay who always kissed up to him."

"You smashed his headlights on the way out of work, Tom. I don't think that was blowing it out of proportion," Wayne said.

Tom bit his lower lip as he read the printout of the charges in front of him.

"Well, it doesn't look good for you Tom. You have a record and a temper, as well as a history of lashing out at those that you disagree with. What would make me think you wouldn't have lashed out at Sebastian Crow?"

"What's this about?" Tom asked.

Instead of answering Tom's question, Wayne asked in a more serious tone, "Where were you last night Tom?"

"I had to drive into the city to pick up a package," Tom explained, hesitatingly.

"Can anyone vouch for you?" Wayne asked making a note in his file of Tom's response.

"No, I was alone. Why?" Tom's voice shook and he forced his voice to sound calm for the first time since they entered the room.

"Sebastian was killed at some point last night," Wayne finally revealed.

"And you think I did it?!" Tom panicked. "Oh, man. I never did nothing to ever hurt anyone. Ever. No matter what I thought about that crazy old man I would never have killed him."

Kerry turned her focus to the cut on Tom's arm, "How did you cut your arm?"

"I was cutting a fishing line loose and the knife slipped," Tom explained.

Wayne glanced at Kerry.

"We are going to need that knife, Tom," Wayne said. "And you're going to need a lawyer."

CHAPTER 6

Tom's alibi was difficult to corroborate, and his lawyer seemed less than interested in offering more information than necessary on his whereabouts. Tom Pruitt drove a '97 GMC Sierra and had no tracking device on it because of its age. Tom, also, was apparently one of the few people left who didn't use a cell phone, making it impossible to track his positioning through GPS on a cell service.

"He won't tell you who he met with in the city?" Kerry asked confused. "Does he not know he is up against a murder charge?"

"My guess is that he was doing something illegal and doesn't want to be in trouble for that," Wayne surmised.

"Can't be worse than a murder charge," Kerry said.

"Did you get the knife?" Wayne asked.

Kerry nodded her head, "Sophia is making the cast now and I will compare it to the ones I took of the wounds later today. But at first glance, it looks like it could be the same knife that was used to stab Sebastian Crow."

"I'm not going to lie, I would love to wrap this case up quickly," Wayne admitted. "That island gives me the creeps and the less time I need to spend out there, the better."

"We still want to search the area for physical evidence that Tom was there. You know what a zoo these murder charges can end up being. We want to have solid physical evidence," Kerry said.

"More than a knife?" Wayne said.

"Yes, if possible."

Sally excused herself as she approached Wayne's desk, "Sorry to interrupt you, but I thought you'd want to know. One of the officers who was canvassing the stores along the main strip recalled Mr. Crow having a heated argument with another man."

"Any idea who he was arguing with? Or what about?" Wayne asked, hoping for a solid lead.

"The only description the officer could get was that he was an older man, and about the same age as Sebastian Crow," Sally read directly from the notes she took just a short while earlier from her call with the officer. "And, that Mr. Cromwell thought it was the boat mechanic who used to work out at Craven's Boat Yard."

"The small shop just outside of town?" Wayne asked.

Kerry had never heard of Craven's Boat Yard and when she asked Wayne, even he thought it had closed years ago.

"I didn't know anyone used that place anymore," Wayne said.

"Well, Mr. Cromwell recognized him as the same mechanic who used to work on his father's boat. He overheard Sebastian and him arguing the day he was killed," Sally said.

"Any idea what they were arguing about?" Kerry asked.

Sally shook her head, "Mr. Cromwell said it seemed personal. Mr. Crow told him to stay out of his business and that it was a private family matter."

"Those were his exact words? A private family matter." Kerry asked.

"Yes. And then Mr. Crow stormed off toward his boat," Sally finished.

"Thanks, Sally. Great job," Wayne said.

When Sally had returned to her desk Kerry turned to Wayne, "If you're so happy about Sally's job why do you look so distraught?"

"Because now we have two suspects, and I have a feeling this case is not going to end anytime soon."

* * *

Early the next morning Kerry agreed to meet Wayne at the station, and they'd go together to see the mechanic at Craven Boat Yard and to see what he and Sebastian were arguing about on the day he was killed. Kerry ended up driving since Wayne's car had suffered a flat at some point after he arrived at work and neither of them wanted to wait for the tire to be changed before they went to speak with the mystery mechanic.

The gravel road from the highway would have easily been missed if Wayne hadn't been familiar with the area. Trees had long overtaken the width of the path and it was evident with each branch that scratched the sides of Kerry's Jeep that not many cars traveled down this road. The Jeep bounced through the potholes that formed from the rain and snow that washed away portions of the limestone. Grass and weeds shot up through the rocks and at points in the road the gravel had completely been overgrown by moss.

Rusted out boat hulls and abandoned trailers were discarded in the now overgrown bushes that lined the road that led to the clearing where the boat yard's main building was situated.

A faded cement building that doubled as both the workshop and office was smaller than Kerry's entire lab.

The door was closed and by the appearance of the shuttered windows, the building hadn't been operational for several years.

"Are you sure this is the place?" Kerry asked as she brought her Jeep to a stop near the building and parked.

"This is the address on file."

Wayne opened the door and stepped out of the Jeep and walked toward the building and Kerry followed close behind.

What appeared to be once a fully functioning, and somewhat busy, boatyard looked more like a forgotten junk heap. Old rusty boat hulls and covers lay in various states of decomposition and were strewn in random locations around the property. Trees and weeds had grown over and through many of the boats and trailers. The only thing missing, Kerry thought, was a vicious attack guard dog.

Wayne turned the rusty wrought iron handle on the main door of the building and was surprised to find it unlocked. An overwhelming smell of dust and mold escaped when the door was pulled open. Thick dampness from years of uncontrolled humidity and water damage emanated from inside the room. Kerry covered her face with her hand and stepped inside, following behind Wayne's steps.

He toggled the light switch back and forth to no avail.

"The power must have been cut from this place a long time ago," Kerry guessed. "I doubt anyone has even been here for a long time."

Wayne pointed his flashlight at what looked to be the main desk in what was most likely the office and walked toward it. Dusty frames nailed to the wall bragged of a successful business that was alive many years ago. Newly purchased boats along with classic wooden yachts were among the collection of the boat yard's frequent clientele. Now, expensive equipment and boats were getting lost in the overgrowth of the brush and weeds and there were no new customers to service.

"I would have thought this place would have been able to keep up a decent business servicing boats," Kerry said as she surveyed the large stack of yellowed pages of invoices that lay strewn across the desk.

"Ever since the small lock system closed down on the west side of Lake Pines it wasn't easy to get boats to this part of the lake. I bet his business closed down over the course of one summer," Wayne said.

"Any idea what this guy's name is?" Kerry asked.

"The business was registered so long ago that Sally couldn't find the paperwork or any electronic trail. Maybe we'll find something here."

They flipped through old files and papers for the next hour and outside of some signed invoices, there was no trace of the owner's name.

"Here's one that is a little clearer. Maybe we can make out his name with this signature," Kerry handed the faded sheet to Wayne.

He pointed his flashlight at the bottom of the page. "Looks like the name starts with a 'C'. . ."

"Colin. It looks like Colin," Kerry said as she looked down at the page.

"I think you're right. Now we just need to track down Colin and find out what he and Sebastian were arguing about the day Sebastian was killed," Wayne said.

Kerry walked along the wall with the faded photos and noticed the same man in many of the pictures, "This must be him. Colin. And look at this picture." Kerry took the picture off the wall and handed it to Wayne.

"Looks like he's standing in front of a cottage. There are many pictures of the same spot, so there's a good chance that it's his place."

Wayne tucked the photo under his arm, "I think that's all we are going to find here. Doesn't look like he's going to be back anytime soon. Why don't we track down what we can with this photo and invoice?"

Kerry eagerly followed Wayne out of the dusty building.

"I need to get back and see if I can get a match on the knife. If so, then maybe finding this Colin guy is a moot point," Kerry said.

"I hope so."

"What is the likelihood that Tom Pruitt is the killer?" Kerry asked.

"Well, he's a loose cannon, so anything is possible. But, you never know," Wayne pulled open the door to her Jeep as his phone buzzed in his pocket and he reached in and pulled it out. "Hello...you serious?...yeah, I'll be back soon."

"Who was that?" Kerry asked.

"Sally. The grieving Mrs. Crow has arrived at my office and she wants the forensic team off the island by the end of tomorrow," Wayne said. "I had a feeling this case was going to be a pain."

Kerry agreed and in a rare instance, felt mildly sorry for what Wayne had waiting for him back in his office.

She climbed into the Jeep and started the engine. Overhead she could hear the faint cry of three crows that were resting on the bow of a large jack pine as she left the boatyard and drove back into Lake Pines.

CHAPTER 7

Once Kerry dropped Wayne at the police station she headed directly to her lab and was surprised to see Simon waiting out front. But he wasn't alone. Nestled in his arms was the small mound of fur that had been added into their lives.

"This is a surprise," Kerry said as she closed the door to her Jeep and walked toward Simon. The puppy began to whimper once he saw Kerry.

"I need to leave the puppy with you today," Simon said, trying to soften the unwelcome news with a smile.

"Why?" Kerry huffed. "Simon, I have a busy day and my lab isn't exactly the perfect place for a dog."

"He chewed through his kennel cage as I was getting ready for work and then he got hold of the pillow on the couch and, well, there's a mess in our living room," Simon confessed.

"This is why I didn't want a dog Simon," Kerry reached out and took the leash. "We're too busy to take care of a puppy. They're obviously a lot of work and it's not fair to him."

The puppy whimpered as it tried to climb up Kerry's leg.

"I know, but you did say you would give it a bit of time," Simon reminded Kerry of the promise she made after she initially protested his gift. "After a little time with this guy, if you still don't think we should keep him then my sister said she would take him. The boys want a dog anyway."

Kerry did promise Simon and it was the least she could do since it was her birthday gift.

"I'll get a new kennel today," Simon promised, and he kissed Kerry's cheek and left before she had an opportunity to change her mind.

Kerry yelled after Simon as he was climbing into his truck, "You owe me, Simon!"

Simon laughed and waved his arm out the window as he drove away.

Kerry looked down at the small pup who was sitting on her foot and staring up at her and her heart melted. He was cute, it just wasn't the right time.

Kerry tugged the leash and walked the puppy into her office.

Sophia squealed when she saw the black pup bounce into Kerry's office behind her.

"He's so cute!" Sophia crouched down and began to fluff the back of the dog's head with her hand. He quickly responded with a nudge of his nose and a few nibbles of her fingers and she laughed.

"He's only here for today because he chewed through the kennel," Kerry said. "Simon is getting a new one today."

"What's his name?" Sophia had picked up the dog and was cuddling her nose in his ears.

"Doesn't have one yet. I'm still not sure if we are going to keep him," Kerry admitted and then changed the subject. "Did you get the lab work completed?"

Sophia put the puppy down on the ground and turned her attention back to her work, "Yes, everything is ready in the lab. I'm just running out to pick up some supplies that we need. I'll be back in a little while."

"Take the afternoon Sophia. You've done a lot of extra work on this case and I have a feeling I'm going to be needing extra help over the next week."

"Are you sure?" Sophia gleefully asked.

"Yes. Go!" Kerry said with a smile.

Sophia thanked her, grabbed her coat, and left.

Kerry tied the leash to the back of her chair and grabbed a coat from her locker and balled it up in a mound that slightly resembled a dog bed. The pup climbed in the center of the nest and Kerry got straight to work.

Sophia had prepared the cast for both the wounds and the knife and Kerry was eager to see if they were a match.

The stab wounds on Sebastian's torso left distinct markings that could be indicative of a hunting or fishing knife. The angle into the body also told Kerry that Sebastian was already laying on the ground when he was stabbed repeatedly. And with no marks on his arms, it was clear he was already dead.

Kerry pulled up the images on her computer and compared the blade dimensions to those of the wounds. They were definitely a match. The other noticeable similarity lay with the pattern of ripping marks along the edges of the wounds that could have been caused by the jagged ridges on the back end of the knife.

Swabs of the knife and blade were taken and after the handle was removed, the dried blood on the inside of the knife was also sampled.

Kerry looked at her watch and wondered how long it would take for the samples to be ready just as the puppy let out a low growl.

"Shush," Kerry whispered to the puppy.

Then she heard the sound that caught the dog's attention and it was coming from the back room. She turned her head and looked behind her and didn't see anything.

"Sophia?" Kerry called out. Although she gave her the afternoon off, she thought maybe Sophia forgot something or was still packing up.

Once there was no answer, Kerry quietly pushed her chair back and walked to the room in the back. She looked through the small window of her office door into the front lobby and saw it was empty. Once again, she heard the sound of metal on metal, and this time, she realized it was coming from the lab.

She let out a sigh knowing it was probably Sophia wanting to help out a little more with the case before she left. Kerry thought she was working too hard and she didn't want her to miss out on the perfect weather today. She went straight into the lab and was going to tell her she had to take the afternoon off. Even if she had to walk her out the door herself.

Kerry pushed open the door, "Sophia, I told you that . . . Hey! What the hell are you doing in here?"

Kerry came face to face with Dave Griffins. Working for the Lake Pines Daily News gave Dave the impression that he was a leading national reporter, when in fact, the largest story he had covered over the last couple of years was the opening of the bakery on Second Avenue.

"I asked you a question?" Kerry grabbed Dave's arm and pulled him out of the lab.

Luckily, he hadn't located where Sebastian's body was being held and he hadn't been near the evidence in the next room. At least from what she could tell.

The last thing she wanted was for him to taint any evidence she had on the table.

Dave Griffins was shorter than Kerry, and at least ten pounds lighter. He had an unapproachable personality and in place of a smile, he wore a permanent smirk. His pale blue eyes sat small on his face and faded easily into his dull skin. The shock of red curly hair on the top of his head was the only color that was easily visible on Dave Griffins in a crowd and right now stood in grave contrast to the crisp white walls and stainless-steel equipment in Kerry's lab.

"Hey, take it easy," Dave tried to wiggle free from Kerry's grasp as she pushed him through the door.

"You're trespassing," Kerry dragged him into the front lobby area, then he broke free of her clutch.

"Everyone has a right to know what happened. A member of our community has been murdered and now a killer is on the loose," Dave was rubbing the spot on his arm where Kerry had grabbed him.

"There is not a killer on the loose. And don't go spreading that around either. You're just going to make people scared," Kerry shot back.

"So, the killer has been caught?" Dave asked, in full sleazy reporter mode.

"I didn't say that," Kerry knew she was walking into a trap if she spoke to him any longer.

"Then the killer *is* on the loose," Dave said, emphasizing the word 'is'.

"Get out, or I'm going to call the police," Kerry warned.

"How was Sebastian Crow killed Doctor Dearborne?" Dave asked.

"Get out Dave," Kerry pushed open the front door and waited until Dave Griffins finally walked out.

Just before she closed the door he mumbled, "Don't say I didn't give you an opportunity to go on record."

Kerry was about to respond but instead, she pulled the door shut and twisted the lock on the door.

She returned to her desk and reached into her pocket and pulled out a dog treat.

"Here you go," she opened her hand and the pup eagerly munched the treat off of her palm. "Good boy."

With Dave Griffins out on the street and the door locked and the pup rewarded, she refocused her attention on her paperwork.

It was easy for Dave Griffins to get Kerry agitated. Especially after last winter. He managed to mess with an investigation not once, but twice over the last year.

No matter what, she couldn't let him distract her.

Kerry needed to stay focused on Sebastian Crow and what could have been used to kill him.

CHAPTER 8

Although Kerry had determined that the knife could have been the same weapon used to stab Sebastian, it was not what had killed him. A blow to his neck did that. Finding the perpetrator of the aggressive stabbing would just place someone at the scene more accurately and then hopefully they could tie that person to the murder. That is if she was able to match the knife to Sebastian's wounds. Finding traces of Sebastian's blood on the knife would firmly do that. And even then, Kerry has seen some sharp lawyers wiggle their clients out of murder charges. However, since Tom Pruitt was defending himself in court, she didn't see that being an issue.

She awoke early to find Simon had already left for his shift at the station. He was given the task of tracking down the owner of Craven's Boat Yard and where they could, with any luck, find him. Kerry was hopeful that he would be able to find something, after all, Lake Pines was a small town, and someone had to know something about him.

Kerry had decided to grab a coffee and bagel for Simon on her way to work and drop it off at the station. It would also give her a chance to see if anything was discovered about the owner of the boatyard. But first, she ended up spending fifteen minutes chasing the unnamed puppy around the house as he dashed under the bed with a sock in hopes of enticing some playtime from Kerry. Eventually, Kerry won and the pup landed with some toys, a bowl of water, and a thick fluffy bed inside his new indestructible kennel courtesy of the K9 Unit supply store. And then she was on her way.

"Good Morning! You left so early that I wasn't sure you had a chance to grab something to eat," Kerry handed Simon a coffee and a bag with the toasted bagel.

"Mmm, that smells great. Butter?" Simon asked of the bagel's topping.

"Of course," Kerry answered.

"I know you are going to ask, but, no, I haven't found out anything on the owner of the Boat Yard," Simon said. "But. . .I did get a post office box number where the city hydro bill was being mailed to for Craven's Boat Yard."

Simon handed Kerry the paper with the information he printed out.

"Wayne is trying to get a warrant so we can get the owner's information from the Post Office, but that could take a while," Simon said.

Wayne saw Kerry from the other side of the room and waved as he walked toward her. "Did you find a match for the blood on the knife?" Wayne asked.

"Not yet, the sample should be ready today. I was hoping that you had a name for the boatyard owner," Kerry said.

"No, but when I was getting the warrant this morning for the Post Office box, I found out that there is not one but two addresses having bills directed to the same post box," Wayne said. "The clerk let the information slip. She wanted to know which company I wanted the warrant for since the form's information had to be very specific. I said both and on my copy, she wrote out Craven Boat Yard as well as Gullstone Lodge."

"Do you know where that is?" Kerry asked.

"Yep, I'm heading out there now. Want to come?" Wayne asked.

Kerry agreed to go. She knew that it would be early afternoon before she heard back from the lab, even with the rush on the samples. The sooner they could rule out any other suspects, the sooner they could possibly narrow the charge against Tom Pruitt. He still refused to offer an alibi for his whereabouts on the night that

Sebastian was killed, and his contentious legal battle could have been enough to push him over the edge. And with those two facts combined, it didn't look good for him.

Gullstone Lodge was twenty minutes from town and once they arrived, they realized was only called that for posterity's sake and not because it was a functioning fishing camp. A small outboard was tied to the dock and Kerry could see the tinge of a light shining from inside the small rustic cottage.

The early morning sun shone on the front of the cottage and reflected off the large front windows. The property appeared as if it was cared for at a basic level. Which meant it looked like it had been regularly mowed, cleaned, and kept clear of fallen trees, but that was where the maintenance chores ended.

The cottage was built in a clearing about fifty feet from the end of the dock. The island was relatively flat, and the building sat at almost at the same level as the dock. A porch wrapped around the cottage and had a wide overhanging roof which would have protected it from both the rain as well as the heat of the sun.

As they walked closer to the cottage Kerry could see that the paint had faded from a dark blue to a light gray and had begun to crack along the edges of the boards.

White trim, yellowed from the elements, edged the window frames of the cottage.

Wayne knocked on the screen door as Kerry and Simon stood on the steps of the porch. There was no response. Wayne knocked again, this time a little harder. The flimsy frame of the screen door bounced against the door jamb echoing each knock.

They waited a short while and after there was no response, Wayne opened the door and called inside.

"Hello, is anyone here?" Wayne stepped inside. "It's Constable Burgess of the Lake Pines Police Department, is anyone home?"

Kerry and Simon followed behind Wayne and stepped inside the cottage. A low beat played from the next room with intermittent sounds of static.

"Sounds like a radio playing in the back room," Wayne called out ahead as he walked to the back of the cottage.

As she followed behind, Kerry recognized the station as the public broadcast from Lake Pines. She was surprised that there was any signal or reception this far from town.

Wayne knocked on the closed door at the end of the hall and announced who he was, once again. When there was no answer, he turned the handle and opened the door.

And on the brown leather armchair sat the presumed owner of Craven Boat Yard and the man who was seen arguing with Sebastian Crow the day he was killed.

He was about the same age as Sebastian Crow, possibly within a few years of Sebastian's sixty-five. He was a rugged man with thick silver hair that was matted down along the edges, revealing where a hat had been worn for many hours of his day. He was a strong-looking man with solid hands but had a medium-built frame. His eyes were closed but if Kerry had to guess they would have been gray or light blue to match his skin tone.

In the center of his shirt were the burnt frayed edges of the single gunshot wound that had taken his life as well as any chance for answers they were hoping to get from him today.

Kerry let out a frustrated sigh as Simon called in the murder to the station.

CHAPTER 9

Kerry left Wayne and the forensic team at the victim's cottage to complete their investigation and headed back to her lab. She took an initial assessment of the victim and was able to determine he was killed sometime between ten last night and six this morning. She would have a more accurate time once the body was in her lab. There were no signs of a struggle or theft, so again the murder was specific as well as personal.

Simon was sure to have a fewer problems now determining the name of the victim along with any information he could obtain on the boatyard. He dropped Kerry at her office before he headed back to the station.

"I'll let you know what I find out," Simon promised as he drove away from the curb.

They were now back to one viable suspect for the murder of Sebastian Crow and by now the lab should have returned the results on the blood found on Tom Pruitt's knife.

Sophia was waiting for Kerry when she walked into her office, "I just received a call from the forensics team. They are bringing another body into the lab!"

Kerry nodded. This was turning out to be an educational summer for Sophia.

"What happened?" She asked.

"A gunshot to the chest. We still don't have a name for the victim, but I'm sure we will by this afternoon," Kerry tossed her purse on her desk.

"I'm going to catch up on some of my emails. Call me when the body arrives," Kerry left Sophia on her own, knowing she was fully capable of getting the lab ready for the arrival of the next body.

Sophia went to the back room to prepare the area for the victim's body which was due to arrive in a couple of hours and Kerry checked her computer for an email from the lab.

As she scanned her inbox, an email from Sally caught her attention. It contained the report from the child services department on the accusation made by Kyle's gym teacher of suspected physical abuse.

Kerry hesitated to open the email. Memories of the case from Montreal came flooding back to her. It wasn't so much the facts of the case that haunted Kerry, but the emotional toll it took on her because of the outcome. She knew she could never face that kind of pain again. The guilt was still too strong.

It was what prompted her to leave Montreal in the first place. It was after she found some solace after a rest in Lake Pines that she was fated to stay and become the town's coroner. No matter how far back the memory stayed, the pain stretched and followed her to Lake Pines.

Kerry's finger double-clicked the email, giving up any choice she had in reading the email regarding the accusations against Sebastian Crow.

The forms were similar across Canada, and Kerry's eyes knew where to scan to find the summary of the charges that were filed.

Bruises and marks that resembled burn scars were noticed by the gym teacher when he was present in the boy's locker room when Kyle was changing into his volleyball uniform.

Mr. Watson, Kyle's gym teacher, knew the signs too well having had a best friend who was the target of abuse from his father. He would cower in the corner as he changed, and didn't mingle with the other boys as they finished their workout. And as they were all eager to peel off their polyester uniform shirts that stuck uncomfortably to their skin after a game, Kyle often grabbed his bag and ran out the door, saying he preferred to change at home.

It was completely by chance that Kyle had decided to change in the locker room after a game when Mr. Watson walked in and noticed the tell-tale bruising. When he asked Kyle about them, he stammered some sort of excuse about falling off his bike and then said he had to get home.

His teacher had no other choice but to report the incident to the principal who, in turn, reported it to the social services department.

With no signs of an inadequate home, and no corroboration from either Kyle or his sister or mother, the report was filed away, and no formal charges were laid.

Kerry sat back in her chair and winced. The thought of a parent making the unspeakable choice to harm their child was incomprehensible to her. And she held no room in her mind, or her heart, for the forgiveness of someone who could be so evil to do such a thing.

Momentarily she wondered if she could continue to search with Sebastian Crow's killer with equal vigor knowing the harm he may have afflicted on his children.

One thing Kerry knew for sure was that she couldn't have another incident like the one from Montreal happen again. No matter what.

She closed the email and began to search the other unread emails that were waiting in her inbox.

Second from the top was an email from the lab with information on the blood swabs from the knife. It was flagged as important and Kerry hoped that they were able to find something on the blade that could connect Tom Pruitt to Sebastian Crow.

Kerry's hopes were soon dashed as she read the lab report. None of the samples matched Sebastian's blood. The samples were run twice and both times the results came back the same. Along with traces of Tom Pruitt's blood cells, there were matches to only corroborate Tom's story that the knife was used while he was fishing. One part of Tom Pruitt's admission was true, he obviously pierced himself with his own knife, and since it wasn't wiped clean, Kerry was satisfied that it couldn't have been used to stab Sebastian.

Even though Tom Pruitt had a motive to kill Sebastian Crow, they didn't have any proof.

Kerry was just about to call Wayne to let him know the results from the lab when Sophia walked through the door.

"The gunshot victim from the island is here Doctor Dearborne. They're earlier than I thought they'd be, but the room is ready," Sophia went back into the lab and escorted the team with the body and instructed them where to place it.

Kerry put her phone back on her desk and decided to call Wayne later. Now she had to perform an autopsy on the last remaining suspect they had in the murder of Sebastian Crow.

CHAPTER 10

Isobella Crow, now Isobella Frank, looked as she sounded on the phone. She was a tall, thin woman, but not scrawny. She had a delicate bone structure that gave her a sense of grace and lightness as she walked. Her auburn hair was pinned back into a loose bun at the base of her neck and a thick beaded necklace hung from her neck.

Light beige linen pants swayed around her legs as she walked, and a thin but contrived smile eked through her tight lips.

She had arrived at the police station just after Wayne returned, and was insisting on knowing when the police tape and search teams would be off Crow Island.

"I need to deal with these matters soon Officer," Isobella said.

"Constable," Wayne corrected her.

"Pardon me?"

"It's Constable, not Officer," Wayne murmured.

"Does it matter?" Isobella asked condescendingly.

Wayne shook his head and began to fumble with some pages on his desk.

"Are you any closer to being finished, *Constable*?" Isobella asked.

"No Ms. Frank. We need to search the area around the cottage for any signs of who may have been there the night your husband was killed," Wayne clenched his jaw waiting for her to correct him on referring to Sebastian as her husband, but it never came.

"Do you have any idea who killed Sebastian?" Isobella asked, softening her tone slightly.

"No, not yet. But we have a suspect who is of interest to us. That's why we need to search for more proof. Give us a couple of days and we will be gone," Wayne said.

"Fine, but no more, please. It's painful to have to deal with all this," Isobella said.

At first, Wayne thought she was talking about Sebastian's death, but realized Isobella was referring to settling the estate.

Not long after Isobella left, Wayne called Kerry to find out about the results from the lab on Tom Pruitt's knife.

"Hey Wayne, I was going to call you earlier but the gunshot victim from the island showed up sooner than I thought," Kerry said.

"Did you start the autopsy on him?" Wayne asked.

"I'm finished. He was killed by a single gunshot wound to the chest. I was able to narrow down the time of death to between midnight and one in the morning," Kerry explained. "The bullet was from a rifle, probably an old hunting one."

"We found the gun. It was in the bush next to the cottage. The killer obviously tossed it on their way back to the dock. I had it dusted for prints, but right now all that we were able to find were the victim's prints on the gun," Wayne said.

"So, we have a murder victim with no weapon and a partial print at the scene and another with the weapon and no print?" Kerry said.

"That's about it," Wayne said. "Please tell me you found something on the knife."

"Sorry. There was no trace of Sebastian's blood on the knife," Kerry said. "Although, it is definitely the same kind of knife that was used to stab him."

"That's a common knife, so I'm not surprised by that. It means we have nothing to warrant us focusing on Tom Pruitt, but I'll have an officer keep an eye on him nevertheless."

Wayne had just ended his call with Kerry when another rang through to his desk.

"Hello, Constable Burgess," Wayne announced.

"Wayne, it's Laura Martin. How are you?"

Laura Martin was the head of the Tourism and Business Committee on the Lake Pines city council and his mother's close friend. She was singlehandedly responsible for enticing two large national companies to set up a satellite office in Lake Pines as a testbed for further investment in the area. There was speculation that she had two other companies poised to make a similar move into the area which was good news for the local economy. And the residents of Lake Pines eagerly got behind any promotion of welcoming a business run by someone other than a bank or the government.

"Hello Laura, how can I help you?"

"It's about the murder case you are working on right now. The one for Sebastian Crow," Laura directed into the phone.

"Yes, what about it?" Surely there was no way that Laura Martin, the leader of his mother's bridge group had any information on who the killer was.

"You just have to shut this down!"

"Excuse me?!" Wayne said.

"You may be too young to remember, so I'll excuse the fact you don't know. But that Sebastian Crow was a terrible man," Laura declared. "He beat his children, who ended up running away, and then his wife eventually ran off scared!"

Wayne didn't know a lot about Sebastian and Isobella, but running scared was not how he would have described her.

"Laura, with all due respect, we have a job to do. And that job is to find out who killed Sebastian Crow and bring them to justice," Wayne stated. "Now, if you'll just let us do our job, I'm sure we'll be done before you know it. So, unless you have any proof or information that is specific to finding the killer. . ."

"Wayne, do you know how bad this can look? I'm this close to closing a deal with two large national companies to move here, and if there is any news of our small town supporting a child abuser then we can kiss those deals goodbye!"

"Finding a killer is not supporting a child abuser, and for that matter, there were never any charges brought against Sebastian. We have a little saying here, 'innocent until proven guilty'. It's how we do our job."

"Ask around Wayne, you'll find there are a lot of people who feel he got what he deserved!" Laura barked before slamming the phone down on her end.

Wayne hung up his phone and grabbed his hat. He needed to go out to Crow Island himself and hurry things along. If they were going to catch Sebastian Crow's killer, then they needed to find some evidence. And if they didn't find it soon, Isobella's lawyers were going to force them off the island, and now Laura Martin was intent on having the investigation closed.

And then there was the unnamed gunshot victim they found this morning.

One thing Wayne knew for sure, it was more than a coincidence that the man seen arguing with Sebastian Crow had also turned up dead. And if he was able to find Sebastian Crow's killer, he was sure the same person would also be found responsible for shooting the man at the cottage called Gullstone Lodge.

CHAPTER 11

Wayne rushed into the station and hurried over to Simon's desk. He called Kerry and told her to meet him at his office. The forensic team found a boot print in the mud near the dock at Gullstone Lodge and when Wayne was at Crow Island the team there found a partial heel print that he hoped would match.

"We may have the evidence we need that may link these two murders," Wayne tossed his hat on his chair and walked over to Simon's desk.

"Any news on the gunshot victim's name?" Wayne asked.

Simon tapped his pen against the side of his computer, "I should hear back from Sally soon. She is pulling the tax records now."

"Constable," a young officer called from behind them. "I have the results for both boot prints."

"And?" Wayne asked.

"They're a match," the officer beamed.

Wayne let out a deep sigh, "Now we just need to find the boot and we have our killer for both murders."

"If we knew what they were arguing about on the day that Sebastian died, we may have a better idea of how to find the killer," Simon suggested. "Maybe we should get Mr. Cromwell in here for another interview or to even look at some mugshots?"

"It's worth a shot," Wayne said.

Simon's phone rang just as Wayne was walking back to his desk and he stopped when he realized it was Sally calling.

Simon nodded as Sally spoke, and Wayne stood watching, hoping to figure out what she was saying. Simon hung up the phone and stared blankly at Wayne.

"You'll never guess who the gunshot victim is," Simon said. "First of all, his name is not Colin, it's Calvin. Calvin Crow. He's Sebastian's brother."

* * *

Kerry arrived at the station surprised to find the victims were related and pleased that a boot print was able to be pulled from both locations.

"So, if we find the boot, we find the killer," Kerry said.

"We just need to narrow down the make and size of the boot and then we can start canvasing some stores in town," Wayne said. "And as for the print, it was a partial, so unless we can find one on record to match it with, we are out of luck."

Wayne's phone rang and he reached out and picked up on the first ring, "Hello, Constable Burgess. . .Yeah, just a minute." Wayne held the phone toward Kerry. "It's for you."

Kerry took the phone, "Hello," Kerry wondered who was calling her on Wayne's number.

"Doctor Dearborne, I'm glad I found you," It was Sophia. "I have been trying to reach you. You left your phone on your desk here."

Kerry patted her pocket, "Shoot, sorry about that. What's the problem?"

"The lab came back with a result for the bloody partial fingerprint that was found at the crime scene. They called a little while ago. They wanted you to know they were sending a report to you," Sophia explained. "I know you were eager to discover what they found."

"You're right. I was," Kerry said. "Can you send it over to Constable Burgess' office? His email is in my contact information."

"Right away," Sophia said.

Wayne opened his email and within a few seconds, a ping alerted him of the new message in his inbox. He clicked the link and opened the file.

"Jackpot," Wayne said. "The blood is the victim's, which we already knew. Since the print was small and smudged, there wasn't much to go off, but what was left was clear enough for a match. It belongs to a Devon Kozlowski."

"Great, let's get him in here," Kerry said. "I for one would love to have these two murder investigations closed."

"It may be easier to find him than you think," Wayne said.

"Why's that?" Kerry asked.

"He's already in prison," Wayne stood and grabbed the keys from the corner of his desk. "He was arrested at four this morning for a break and enter at the pharmacy. Why don't we go talk to Devon now?"

Kerry followed Wayne out of the station and to where his car was parked on the street.

"Looks like it was a robbery gone bad after all, Doctor Dearborne," Wayne chuckled as he opened the driver's side door and slid behind the wheel.

Kerry still wasn't convinced. There was more to the murder, she was sure of it.

CHAPTER 12

Simon drove ahead in his own car and was waiting on the front steps of the prison when Wayne pulled up. They were going to interrogate Devon and hopefully fill in the missing pieces of the night that Sebastian Crow was murdered and close the case quickly. They may also be able to close the case on Calvin Crow as well, which Wayne hoped they could do.

"It's not that often that our suspect is already in prison," Wayne joked with Simon as they walked up the steps toward the front door.

He dropped Kerry off at her office on the way to the prison so she could get Sebastian prepared for both Isobella and Katrina. No matter how long they had been apart, they were going to see Sebastian for the last time, and she wanted to make it as easy on them that she could.

"So, you're telling me that Sebastian is still married?" Simon asked.

"Weird, huh?" Wayne said. "Hasn't seen either of his kids too. Do you remember his son at all?"

Simon shook his head, "No. You?"

"No, and he would be a little younger than us. Strange in a town this small that I wouldn't remember him."

Wayne signed him and Simon in at the front desk and informed the supervisor why they needed to speak with Devon Kozlowski, the young boy recently arrested for robbery.

"He's been a busy boy," the supervisor handed Wayne and Simon their card passes. "I will have him brought into room two for you guys."

"Thanks," Wayne snapped the visitor's badge on his shirt and walked to the interrogation room that was marked with a large number two.

Simon and Wayne waited less than five minutes for the prisoner to be brought into the room. Footsteps echoed in the hall as the guard and prisoner approached the interrogation room. Their steps echoing off the linoleum floor as they made their way down the twenty-foot-long hall from the prison's door.

The guard opened the door and then stepped to the side to let Devon Kozlowski walk through before him. Devon sat in the empty chair and then the guard handcuffed him to the desk, leaving him to be questioned by Wayne and Simon.

Devon was a rough-looking man. But not the large, buffed type. He was scrawny and pale. He lacked the muscle tone that most men his age would have and wore an angry scowl, as Wayne quickly surveyed his body language. His eyes were a deep, dark brown. Almost black and they had a blank stare. He was the kind of guy that if you met him in a bar you would think he was looking for a fight.

"I didn't do it," Devon snapped.

"You don't even know why we are here," Wayne replied.

"That cop that pulled me over last night planted that stuff in my car," Devon shouted. "It wasn't mine."

"Yeah, that's what the report said but yet, here you are," Wayne leaned back in his chair.

"Well it's a load of crap," Devon flipped his hand in the air. "I'm going to fight this."

"I would imagine you would want to," Wayne flattened a sheet of paper on the desk and slid it in front of Devon. "Turns out you were on a short leash with your probation officer. You were already accused of another robbery. If you go down for this, then you are going away for a long time Devon. You have quite the relationship with the police in the three towns you lived in."

Devon didn't need to read the sheet to know what was on it. He had been arrested for robbery, drug possession, and assault. The last few times he was able to convince the judge to release him on his promise to get help with his drug addiction but considering that the arresting officer found a significant amount of oxycodone in his car, likely, he wasn't successful at that.

"I think the case against you is pretty clear Devon," Wayne said. "But I'm not here because of your arrest last night."

"Then why are you here?" Devon demanded.

"Where were you yesterday Devon?" Wayne asked.

"I was here," Devon snapped as he yanked his cuffed arm, shaking the table.

"I mean *before* you were arrested," Wayne clarified.

"I was at home," Devon said.

"Any witnesses?"

"No," Devon darted his eyes from Wayne to Simon. "What's this about?"

"Do you know a man by the name of Calvin Crow?" Wayne asked.

Devon just stared at Wayne and shook his head, no expression revealing any recognition of the name.

Wayne decided to try again.

"Do you know a man by the name of Sebastian Crow?" Wayne asked.

At this, Devon tightened his lips, flattening his back against the chair, and didn't answer.

"We just want to know what happened when you were there," Simon said.

"Where was that?" Devon asked.

"Crow Island," Simon answered. "We found a print of yours in his cottage."

Devon shrugged his shoulders, "Don't know what you're talking about."

"Strange, I'd think you would remember a body covered in blood," Simon said.

Devon's nostrils flared and the muscles on his jaw flexed as he clamped down his teeth, "I think I want to speak to a lawyer."

"Good idea Devon. Because you're being charged with the murder of Sebastian Crow," Wayne proceeded to read Devon his rights and Simon watched the tense look on Devon's face fade to one of disinterest as Wayne laid out the charges before him.

Wayne notified the guard that they were done questioning Devon and that he could be returned to his cell. Simon and Wayne waited in the room as the guard unlocked the handcuffs and walked Devon out of interrogation room number two and back into his cell.

Wayne gathered his paper and said, "What do you think?"

"Guilty as hell," Simon said.

"And."

"And there is no way he did this alone," Simon added. "He is too small to bring down a man as big as Crow without a struggle."

"Exactly what I was thinking. There was someone else in the cottage with Devon when he killed Sebastian Crow."

CHAPTER 13

Devon Kozlowski was charged with the murder of Sebastian Crow, and since he was currently in prison, the judge eagerly moved up the charges on his docket. Wayne was grateful for the fact that Devon was in prison while they concluded their investigation. He knew that he was exactly the type of suspect that would be at risk of disappearing if he was free.

The heavy rain had begun at around nine the night before and continued into the next day. The heavy deluge was a continuation of a rainy spring and summer this season and was quickly testing the patience of the residents and cottagers in the area. It was getting hard to fill rainy days with movies, books, and board games. People were longing to have extended days in the sun, either lounging on the beach or in a chair.

When summer came to Lake Pines people expected to be out on the water. Boating, fishing, and socializing with friends that they hadn't seen since the previous summer.

Right now, the rain was posing a logistical problem for the investigation of Sebastian Crow's murder. The forensic crew set up tents and covers on Crow Island around Sebastian's cottage and boathouse but twice the heavy rain had collapsed a tent that covered the front steps to the cottage, soaking the ground below and destroying any possible evidence of the intruders.

Wayne had picked Kerry up at the Main Street dock and they drove out to Crow Island together to hopefully speed up the investigation.

"Was your crew able to find anything other than the partial boot print that could identify who the intruders were?" Kerry asked. Wayne had pulled into the boathouse and they were able to get the boat out of the rain.

"Not yet. And that's going to be a problem. When Devon was arrested, he was wearing a pair of running shoes, not boots. And a thorough search of his car didn't turn a pair up. The rain has caused a bit of a problem as well, but now we have another issue," Wayne said. "Isobella is insisting that we wrap things up so she can get on with the business of finalizing the estate."

"You're kidding me," Kerry said.

"You can see for yourself," Wayne pointed toward the cottage. "Sally called me and said she has been here all morning. And there's another thing."

"What's that?" Kerry asked.

"She's not positive but Sally thinks she saw Isobella walking around the property with Tom Pruitt earlier today," Wayne said.

"Really?" Kerry asked. "Now what do you think they were talking about?"

"I don't know, but let's keep that under our hats until we can gather more information," Wayne asked Kerry, hoping she would agree.

Kerry pounded up the steps and ran under the tarped tent cover that surrounded the cottage. Sally saw her coming and held open the door as Kerry reached the front steps.

She walked directly over to Isobella who she figured was the striking tall woman with auburn hair. She was sitting by the window in an orange dress looking impatient.

"Do you want to tell me why you are rushing our team on this investigation?" Kerry pointedly asked.

"And you are?" Isobella stood and faced Kerry with a stern look.

"Doctor Dearborne. I'm trying to figure out who killed Sebastian and you rushing our team to finish is not helping," Kerry snapped.

"I thought you arrested someone already? That's what Constable Burgess told me," Isobella said.

"If we are going to make the charges stick then we need to have a solid case to make sure he doesn't get off on a technicality," Kerry explained, thinking of the boot print. "The forensic team needs to go over this place top to bottom, and they don't need you pressuring them to finish."

Kerry could sense the silence in the cottage as every member of the police force and forensic team that was within earshot stopped to listen.

"What's the big hurry anyhow? You didn't even know you were part owner of this island and hadn't spoken to Sebastian for fifteen years," Kerry said.

Isobella folded her arms tightly in front of her chest and let out a deep sigh, "I'm in charge of settling Sebastian's estate, and part of that estate, a huge part, is getting rid of this island. And as it happens, I have a buyer lined up willing to take possession, but he wants it before the August long weekend."

"Really?!" Kerry asked mockingly and then turned to yell at the team within viewing distance. "Then let's clear out guys. There's a buyer."

"There is no need to be sarcastic," Isobella uttered through clenched teeth.

"Yes, there is, mother!" a voice yelled from outside the front door.

Everyone in the room turned to see where the voice came from. On the front step was a woman in her thirties. She was dressed more demurely than her mother and her eyes were lined red from crying. She pulled open the screen door and walked into the cottage.

"Why can't you just let everyone do their job?" Katrina sobbed. "Dad's gone. The least we can do is make sure whoever killed him gets sent to prison. You never cared for this place, or dad, anyhow!"

"That's not true Katrina," Isobella sounded surprisingly defensive and small. "I loved your father and this cottage. We had many great memories here."

"That's not how I remember it," Katrina turned around and stormed away from her mother, and out of the cottage.

Isobella fumbled with her arms and then finally grabbed her bag from the floor and began to walk away. She turned around just as she reached the door, "I'll give you until the end of the week to finish your investigation then I want you all gone. It's time to put everything to rest, once and for all."

Isobella pushed the screen door open and walked down the steps and under the tarp until she reached the dock where her boat was tied up.

"She *really* doesn't understand how this works, does she?" Kerry asked.

"I guess not, but let's try and close this case fast. I have a bad feeling about it dragging on," Wayne said.

Kerry didn't want to admit it, but she did as well.

CHAPTER 14

The forensics team combed the entire area around the cottage and couldn't find any evidence that indicated where Devon and his accomplice entered the cottage. And why they were there in the first place? The tense interaction with Isobella made Wayne neglect to mention that Calvin, Sebastian's brother, had also been killed. They knew that they could be connected but it wasn't clear how. At least not yet.

Lawyers sometimes had less evidence from murder investigations to go into court with, so Kerry felt they could proceed with the bloody fingerprint alone. She really had hoped to find out who else was in the cottage with Devon when Sebastian was killed as well as knowing what really happened that night. She hated the idea of a killer being on the loose in Lake Pines.

By the time Kerry left Crow Island, it was dark. All she could think about was getting home and into a hot bath.

Even though it was early July Kerry felt a chill and she turned up the heat in her car as she drove along the dark stretch of the roadway into town. Wayne did his best to keep them both dry as they traveled out to Crow Island and then back again, but his driving and the tarps were no match for the rain that battered them in the boat. She gave up trying to even cover her head when they arrived at the dock where Kerry had parked her Jeep, and she ran as fast as she could until she was close enough to unlock the doors remotely.

Rain-soaked the driver's seat when Kerry opened the door and climbed inside. The yellow raincoat clung to her back, and her skin began to itch under the layers she wore to keep warm. She leaned forward and pulled her arms out of the coat, pulled her sweater over her head, and tossed them on the back seat. Water dripped from the ends of her hair that hung haphazardly above her shoulders. Each drip felt like a bucket against her already damp neck.

She shook her head from side to side and ran her fingers through her hair, slicking it back and away from her forehead. Steam began to fog up her windows as well as her rear-view mirror. She reached for a paper napkin from her coffee order that morning and wiped the mirror clear only for it to fog up a few minutes later.

With the windshield wipers on full Kerry put the Jeep into drive and began the long drive home. It was already dark and the lights from both the streetlamps and the cars in front of her blurred through the raindrops that streamed in waves across the windshield. She slowed the Jeep and followed the line of traffic in front of her which seemed slower than normal.

She began to think about everything that happened on Crow Island that day. It had upset her how easily Isobella was able to get her to react negatively. She rarely snapped at people and never at a grieving family member. But Isobella wasn't really a family member and she most definitely was not grieving.

In any event, it wasn't a professional way to react and she promised to call Isobella first thing tomorrow and apologize.

Kerry reached her hand toward the control panel and pressed the defog button sending a steady stream of cool air toward the front window and a chill ran over her arms. She couldn't wait to get home.

The blurred red taillights in front of her suddenly brightened and then stopped in their place. A mirage of red and blue lights flashed above the cars in front of her and was distorted through the streams of wavy water running down her windshield. A heavy downpour began to pound on the roof of her Jeep, causing a thunderous echo around her head, drowning out the radio.

A warped figure walked up to the driver's side of the cars lined along the highway and began to instruct each driver to follow the detour arrows along the shoulder of the road.

Kerry lowered her window as the officer approached her car.

"I'm going to need you to follow the arrows and take the detour as it is marked," the officer instructed.

Kerry had to yell over the sound of the pounding rain, "What happened officer? An accident?" God, Kerry hated car accidents.

"No. A mudslide," the offer leaned closer to Kerry's window so she could hear him.

"Aidan?" Kerry barely recognized the officer under the heavy rain gear and umbrella. "You got quite the shift tonight."

"No kidding," the young officer laughed. "I'm surprised you weren't called in tonight."

"Why's that?" Kerry was afraid to ask.

"The mudslide blocked only part of the highway, but it also brought down some bones. That's why the detour was put in place," he explained.

"Any chance they are animal bones?" Kerry asked.

Aidan shook his head, "No there was a femur bone that is visible in the pile of mud."

Kerry's phone buzzed on the seat beside her and she looked over to see Wayne's contact number flash up.

"There's my call now," Kerry said. "Where can I pull over?"

The officer directed Kerry out of the flow of traffic and over to the side of the road where the other emergency vehicles were lined up. She reached into the back of the seat and grabbed her raincoat and pulled it over her chilled arms. The coat was still wet, and the rubbery material clung against her body. Kerry stepped out of her Jeep and pulled up the hood of the coat.

As she walked toward the white spotlight, she could see the outline of three officers that were pulling a roll of yellow police tape around the area. There was almost nothing for Kerry to work on for months and now there were going to be three cases at once in her lab. Then Kerry thought of a phrase her father would use. *When it rains, it pours.* And she couldn't help but laugh at the irony of being soaked as she walked toward the mudslide.

Kerry's phone buzzed inside her pocket. She pulled it out to answer it. It was Wayne calling her again.

"Wayne, I'm at the mudslide now," Kerry yelled into the phone. The echo of the rain and the wind made it difficult to hear – and speak.

"Good, then you know that there are some bones that were found in the debris. Not sure what everything looks like there but it's probably a real mess with all the rain.

Let me know if there is anything I can get for you," Wayne offered.

"Some coverage would be good," Kerry said.

"Most of the tents are on Crow Island," Wayne said. "But let me see what I can do."

"Thanks, Wayne," Kerry said.

"Oh, and I got a call from Isobella's lawyer after you left. They want this wrapped up and us out of here by the end of the week and they are filing a motion in court to make sure we're gone," Wayne said. "That's why I came back out. I'm going to have the forensic team work around the clock here."

"Okay. Thanks for letting me know," Kerry ended the call and slipped her phone back into her pocket. She noticed the battery was at ten percent and soon it would be completely out of power.

"Doctor Dearborne, right this way," Aidan lifted the yellow police tape and stood to the side while Kerry walked underneath.

They had to step through a thick band of mud before they reached the area where the initial bone was found. Branches and rocks protruded from the mud and made digging around the area difficult. A combination of loose gravel and thick gumbo clumped along the edge of the mudslide and blocked a full lane on the road.

The officers had set one of the large spotlights, so it shone directly on the bone that stuck out from the mud. Although the light wasn't great and her vision through the rain was blurred, Kerry could see that the bone that was protruding from the mess was a femur.

"I'm not sure what we are going to be able to find tonight but let's get started," Kerry instructed the group of officers around her.

After a brief set of instructions, each one set out in their designated direction to search for more bones that would help Kerry identify the victim.

There is a set pattern that the mudslide often takes debris. And if these bones were buried together, which they most likely were, then they were probably contained within a short distance of the femur.

Over the first hour of searching the officers and two members of the forensic team were able to locate most of the torso, another leg, and one arm. The rain began to slow then eventually stop, making the search easier for the team.

From the street, Kerry could see streams of lights from the many flashlights that were weaving across the hill as the team searched around the fallen trees and piles of rocks.

She shivered as the wind picked up over the water and blew across the road. Her t-shirt was soaked and felt frozen under the damp raincoat. If she could see her fingertips, she was sure they would be tinged blue by now.

"Doctor Dearborne!" a muffled yell from inside the clump of trees midway up the hill caught her attention.

Kerry began to step over the rocks at the base of the mudslide and walk toward the voice that was calling her.

Three officers were standing around a small piece of ground, all of them shining their flashlights on an item of interest.

"What did you find?" Kerry asked.

Two officers stepped sideways to give Kerry a clear view of what they found.

"Shit! Not what I wanted to see," Kerry said.

Shadows from her body and the officers next to her darkened over the ground. Lights were shining on them from behind and Kerry turned around quickly and was staring into Dave Griffins' face.

The Lake Pines Daily News was small, how did they have a reporter that seemed to be out at all hours of the day! Kerry was nowhere near ready to talk about what they found, and nowhere near ready to deal with Dave Griffins.

"What are you doing here?" Kerry yelled.

The cameraman stood behind Dave, filming the reporter on his tablet. Kerry threw her hand up and tried to block the view of Dave's sidekick who was filming the scene. The officers shone the light in the direction of the tablet making it impossible for him to collect any more footage. Instead, he turned the tablet toward Kerry and zoomed in on her face as she began to yell at Dave.

"I asked you a question!" Kerry yelled. "What are you doing here?"

"I'm reporting on the news," Dave smirked. "That's what we do you know."

"Well, my friends here arrest people, you know, that's what they do."

"You are not trying to block the press are you Doctor Dearborne?" Dave goaded Kerry.

Kerry reached out and grabbed the tablet away from the sidekick, "Get out of here before I really get mad. This is a cordoned off area and you are not supposed to be here. You *are* breaking the law and I'll make sure that you are charged."

Dave held up his hands and backed away, "Doesn't matter, it's all up on the cloud anyway." Dave grabbed his sidekick's arm and pulled him down the hill and toward the van that was parked just outside the yellow police tape.

"I want to know how that clown got in here," Kerry yelled at everyone around her.

The team stood silent as they waited for Kerry to calm down and let them know what to do next.

Kerry rubbed her forehead and closed her eyes. She composed herself and then returned to where she was initially standing when Dave arrived.

"Let's bag this up properly and get it back to my lab with whatever remains we were able to unearth. If anyone can work through the night, great. Otherwise, let's get a team out here tomorrow and start fresh," Kerry turned and began to walk down the hill. "Just make sure the area is guarded and that no more intruders can wander in."

Remains were one thing, but a child's backpack was another. This was turning out to be a horrible summer.

CHAPTER 15

A fitful night of sleep was followed by a painfully cold shower. The hot water tank died at some point over the last twenty-four hours and Simon had left early that morning to get a replacement before he started work. That combined with Kerry's three trips to the backyard throughout the night because the puppy had to go to the bathroom, made her feel like a zombie. Kerry tried to compensate with an extra-strong cup of coffee, and she was slowly feeling more alive.

She arrived in her office and Sophia was fast at work arranging the remains found in the mudslide on the examination table. Kerry dropped her bag in her drawer and noticed that there were three messages on her desk. One from Wayne, another from Isobella's lawyer, and the third from Katrina.

Kerry needed a few hours before she talked to any one of those three people, but she already knew the first would be Katrina and the last would be Isobella's lawyer if she even decided to call him at all.

"Good morning Doctor Dearborne," Sophia was laying out a lab coat and gloves for Kerry.

"Thanks, Sophia," Kerry slipped on the coat and the protective gloves and began her examination.

She knew from the style of the backpack that the remains were most likely that of a child. Once they were displayed on the table, she could see that they were definitely the contents of a teenager's backpack. Enough of the remains had been recovered to determine the age and sex of the victim. As of this morning, the skull had not been found and Kerry knew that dental records would help confirm a positive identity of the young victim.

The remains belonged to a young male and there were numerous cracks and spits in his bones. Some were caused by the mudslide, however, others were caused by trauma from either sports or rough activity but there were no major breaks. The top section of his spine was cracked, and Kerry wanted to investigate the break under a microscope to rule out a possible cause of death.

The break was at the C1–C2 vertebrae and when Kerry magnified the bones, she could tell it was an old break and probably the cause of death.

She gleaned all the information she could from the bones, so she decided to turn her attention to the contents of the backpack that she and Sophia began to lay out across the table. Most of the contents were soaked from the rain and many years under snow, ice, and dirt. The canvas on the navy backpack was worn away with age and what looked like markings of animals clawing at the fabric to get to what was inside.

Dirt-stained shirts, two pairs of pants, and many socks and underwear had been stuffed in the main section of the pack. The small zipper area held a crumpled pile of five and ten dollar bills, a washed-out piece of paper with faded ink, and a dime. Kerry lifted the flap on the back of the pack and unzipped a small pouch. Inside was a key still attached to a brass keychain.

The key was to a house door and the keyring was like one you would find in a kitschy gift store. It was small and round and had the symbol of a crow. A large black crow.

* * *

Kerry crumpled the message that had Isobella's lawyer's name and number scribbled across it and tossed it in the garbage. She dialed Katrina's number and it rang three times before it went to her voice mail. Kerry left her name and number and told Katrina to call whenever she could.

Wayne's call was the next one to return.

"Kerry," Wayne answered her call on the first ring. "What were you able to find out?"

"The remains are those of a young boy, a teenager most likely. There was no i.d. and his pack contained mostly clothes, so possibly a runaway," Kerry explained.

"Unfortunately, we get a lot of those around here," Wayne said. "Anything else?"

"A key and a keychain. It looks like it's a key for a door to a house," Kerry said.

"I can see if we can trace it to a specific lock. I can come to get it, or you can drop it off," Wayne said.

"If you could come to get it, I could finish writing up my report," Kerry suggested. "Oh, and there is something else."

"Yeah, what is it?" Wayne asked.

"Can you also see if you can trace the key chain?" she asked.

"We can try. Put it all in the same bag and I will see what we can do."

Kerry thanked Wayne and turned on her computer so she could complete her report when her phone buzzed again. This time it was Simon.

"Hi, Simon. Please tell me you got the water tank fixed," Kerry had been dreaming of a hot bath since she left the house in the morning.

"Yeah, that's fixed but I'm calling because of something else," Simon hesitated.

"What is it, Simon?" Kerry turned her chair around and faced the window. "Is everything alright?"

"Are you at your computer now?" Simon asked.

Kerry turned her chair back around and faced her computer again, "Uh, huh."

"Go to Channel Four's website," Simon instructed. "You are not going to like it, but you should see it."

Kerry entered the news station's website address before Simon was finished explaining.

"Seems as if Dave Griffins decided to upload your outburst he caught on film to the web," Simon explained.

"How? I grabbed the tablet from his stupid little sidekick," Kerry said. She watched with the volume off as the camera caught her face contorted and angry at the sight of Dave in the search area.

"That's what the cloud is Kerry. Everything that is taped is automatically uploaded and backed up to a remote system so even if the phone, tablet, or whatever is lost or damaged, you still have the footage," Simon said.

"Great, how wonderful," Kerry dropped her face into the palm of her hands.

"I know he shouldn't have been there, but you need to not let that idiot push your buttons," Simon said. "It just gives him the opportunity to gloat and you end up looking bad."

"I know Simon. I had just found the kid's backpack when he crept up behind us. He caught me off guard," Kerry closed the window on her computer.

"What are you going to do now?" Simon asked.

Kerry was about to answer Simon's question when another call came in on her phone. She pulled the phone away from her ear and saw that it was Peter calling her.

"Shoot. I need to go Simon. Peter is calling and I don't think it's going to be good."

Simon wished her luck. Kerry thanked him and then disconnected their call and then took a deep breath before she answered the call from her supervisor, Sergeant Peter George.

CHAPTER 16

Kerry listened to Peter list the reasons why she needed to learn how to control her temper and how she should assume that at any given time she is being watched. She knew he was right and now that he was her supervisor, she knew he had to address her recorded outburst.

"It's not the fact you yelled at Dave, you were completely in the right to protect your crime scene and he was trespassing. Unfortunately, the issue is purely political. If we are going to seem like a competent detachment and ensure we have the citizen's trust, we always need to look professional," Peter explained.

"And Dave and his redheaded sidekick? Do they have to answer for their actions?" Kerry asked.

Peter laughed, "I already spoke with their editor and both have been put on suspension for one week."

"Really?" Kerry asked, more shocked than curious.

"I guess the threat of obstruction of justice and being charged with disturbing a crime scene got their attention," Peter said. "Look, you are going to be busy with all of these cases. Are you going to be able to handle them?"

"You know I can Peter," Kerry promised.

"Just thought I'd ask," Peter said. "How is Wayne making out?"

"Pretty good. I think he may be getting the hang of the job," Kerry joked.

"Ha! About time. Call if you need anything, okay." Peter said.

"I will," Kerry ended the call and returned her focus to writing her report on the recent remains.

As she typed, she hoped that not many people would see the video that Dan Griffins uploaded to the web, but she had a bad feeling that it was going to come back to haunt her.

* * *

The common area in the prison was split into two zones. One on the outside, and the other on the inside of the building which was larger since it was used for much of the year. The rain was continuing to batter Lake Pines and the yard had become muddy and soaked. Even though the rain had subsided for the day, most of the prisoners opted to use the inside space for their recreation time.

Devon grabbed a deck of cards from the guard and walked over to a vacant table at the far end of the room. Devon often kept to himself and deliberately didn't try and mingle with any of the inmates. He knew he wasn't the ideal citizen, by the police department's standards, but he also knew that getting involved with most of the guys in the Lake Pines prison would not be in his best interest. One misstep with any of them and he'd be done for life.

He shuffled the cards and kept his head low. He started to place seven cards in a row on the table and began to layer them for a hand of solitaire. He'd be doing a lot of this if those cops get their way and slap a murder charge on him. It wasn't supposed to happen this way. He cursed himself for the rashness in which he reacted.

But it was too late to change what happened. Now he had to figure out a way to get out of this mess, and fast.

Devon was trying to focus on the cards he was flipping from the deck in his hand, but the noise in the room was getting louder. Finally, the chatter drew Devon's attention away from the cards on the table over toward the crowd that was congregating at the far end of the room.

"Turn it up," yelled one inmate, that was too small to see over the men standing in front of him.

"It's that idiot reporter!" yelled another.

"My brother went to school with him, he was always kissing up to everyone, but no one liked him."

A loud burst of laughter came from the group.

The crowd was gathered around the lone television that hung suspended from the ceiling, four feet above the highest reach of any of the inmates. It was bolted to a thick steel arm and fastened to a beam after a fight broke out and a group of angry inmates began destroying the room. Or so Devon was told by the guy being held in the cell next to him. Devon just listened to him talk all night and didn't participate in the conversation. Eventually, he stopped talking and went to sleep.

Devon had no interest in making friends or owing anyone any favors, but the opportunity to gather any amount of intel was always valuable.

The scene on the screen grabbed Devon's attention and he stopped dealing himself cards and leaned back in his chair and listened to the video that was being aired.

The familiar hill stole Devon's breath away as he focused on what both the reporter and the woman, he was arguing with, were saying.

"Is it true that the mudslide took down a body here?" the reporter asked.

"How did you get in here?" the woman screamed. She pushed him aside and began to yell at both him and the guy taping.

Devon didn't know who she was, but she was no-nonsense and obviously upset at finding the two reporters in the area.

Under the image of the woman some text scrolled across the screen. *Doctor Kerry Dearborne, Lake Pines Coroner confronts reporter Dave Griffins.*

"Is it true? Were bones found in the mudslide tonight?" Dave peppered his questions at her.

However, it was the last question the reporter was able to ask. The women reached out and grabbed hold of the video and it fluttered before it cut to black.

He would have liked to say he almost forgot about that hill, but it would have been a lie if he did.

That day was cemented in his mind. It was the worst day of his life. Taking the life of a friend is not something you do and easily forget about. He could still remember the feel of his hand against his neck and the sound of the snap that came with the one single movement.

He buried him as deep as he could and left the backpack as both a reminder as well as some sort of tombstone that only he would know existed. Now it may be the one way he could get out of here and he knew exactly who to call.

But before he could figure out how to contact her, a guard yelled from across the room, "Kozlowski! You have a visitor."

CHAPTER 17

"What do you mean he said I assaulted him?" Kerry gasped. She held the stapled pages in her hands and flipped them back and forth hoping she misread the claim.

"Griffins said you used unnecessary force to remove him from the area. He also said that the area was not blocked off and that he was free to access the mudslide," Peter had driven in from Thunder Bay when Dave Griffins' lawyer delivered his intention to sue to the main dispatch office. And since Sergeant Peter George was her superior, as well as the superior of everyone involved with the case, it was delivered directly to him.

"That's a load of crap and you know it," Kerry snapped. She tossed the sheets on her desk. "Each of those officers had not only made sure the area was secure, but they were also taking care to reroute traffic around the mudslide. Every single protocol was followed."

"I have no doubt that they were. The problem is now we have to prove it," Peter said.

"And how are we going to do that?" Kerry asked. "We are in the middle of not one, not two, but three investigations. Are we supposed to drop everything to deal with Griffins' lawsuit?"

Peter shrugged, "We have to address this. There is no option."

"But five million dollars? Really?" Kerry quipped. "I would've tossed him off the hill if I thought we were going to be sued that much."

"See, that's exactly how *not* to react and what *not* to say," Peter said. "Especially if someone may be recording you."

"I know. I know. I'm just venting to you," Kerry said.

"We are going to fight this Kerry so just be cooperative with our lawyers, please. It will go a lot smoother if you do," Peter pleaded. "And whatever you do, don't speak with Griffins."

"Don't worry, I won't," Kerry promised.

"There's one more thing," Peter said.

"Yes?" Kerry waited for the reprimand to stay away from social media, but that wasn't what her supervisor, and her friend, was going to say.

"I want you to step back from the investigations. Just for a while," Peter said.

"Are you serious?" Kerry roared.

"Just the part where you seem to make yourself noticeable to the public," Peter explained. "The less chance of Griffins or his team catching you in a position where they can put you in a bad light, the better."

"Then what am I supposed to do? Sophia is too inexperienced to run the lab on her own," Kerry snapped.

"Stay in the lab. I'm not saying to stay out of the investigation, just out of Dave Griffins' line of sight. At least until this case is over."

Peter put his hand on Kerry's shoulder, "It's going to be okay. Lawsuits like this are something we are prepared to deal with. You just focus on helping Wayne with these investigations by giving him all the evidence you can find and let us do our job."

Kerry thanked Peter and walked him to the door. After he left, she sat in her chair and stared at the pages that she tossed on her desk earlier and she reached out and grabbed hold of them again.

"Five million," she mumbled.

A buzzing sound echoed from inside her pocket and distracted her attention away from Griffins' lawsuit to answer her phone. Without seeing who the call was coming from Kerry answered on the second ring.

"Hello."

"Doctor Dearborne?" a deep raspy voice asked.

"Speaking," Kerry answered.

"It's Officer Richards at the Lake Pines jail. I'm calling because one of our prisoners has requested to speak with you," he said.

"Really? Who would that be?" Kerry asked.

"Devon Kozlowski."

"The guy who's being charged with the murder of Sebastian Crow?" Kerry asked.

"That's the one," Officer Richards said.

Kerry looked down at the pages outlining the lawsuit that had been launched against her, "I don't think that'll be a good idea. Tell him if he has anything to share to go directly to his lawyer."

"He doesn't have one yet," Officer Richards explained.

"Then maybe you should tell him it would be a good idea to have one. After all, he's going up against a murder charge," Kerry said.

"I'll let him know," Officer Richards said.

"Okay, thanks," Kerry was about to end the call when Officer Richards interjected.

"And by the way, everyone here backs you up on that Griffins jerk. You were completely in your right to do what you did. It's guys like that who end up tainting an investigation and then end up blaming us for not being able to solve it!"

Kerry thanked Officer Richards and felt slightly better after having spoken to him.

Kerry put her phone down on the desk and decided to walk to Joe Blacks and get a large latte and ten minutes of fresh air.

When she stepped onto the sidewalk and locked the office door, she couldn't hear her phone ring or see that it was Katrina trying to reach her for the second time.

Katrina began to leave a message but instead, she decided she needed to speak with her mother first. After that, she would call Doctor Dearborne and tell her everything.

* * *

Simon was at Joe Blacks getting coffee for himself and some Officers when he spotted Kerry at the counter.

"I would have brought you a coffee. You should've called," Simon said.

"I needed the fresh air," Kerry explained. "Peter was by to see me earlier."

"I heard he was in town. It's the lawsuit isn't it?" Simon asked.

"Does everyone know?" Kerry asked.

"Just the department," he explained. "But everyone is on your side."

"Well, I'm not sure that will help, but thanks," Kerry grabbed her order and she and Simon walked outside and sat on the bench in front of the café.

"It's just super frustrating dealing with a lawsuit on top of the cases," Kerry popped the lid off her coffee and took a long drink.

"There's insurance for lawsuits like this. It's not going to affect your job either, so try and put it out of your mind," Simon said.

"I'll try," Kerry promised.

"I know you don't like to watch the video he uploaded, but there are over ten thousand views already, and, every single comment is one backing you up. Everyone thinks Griffins was a jerk for what he did," Simon said.

"Really?" Kerry said.

Simon grabbed his phone and swiped the lock screen, "Look."

He pressed the saved link on his phone and pulled up the video stream that contained the shot that Griffins and his videographer took on the mudslide. Underneath the video was the counter tallying the total number of views and likes. Below that, all the comments Simon was referring to were posted. Hordes of viewers across the country voicing their support of Kerry.

Along the side were videos relating to Griffins' taping. Montages of his other reports that were equally aggressive as well as some bystanders that were filming their altercation at the site.

Kerry caught a glimpse of one that interested her the most.

"Play the fifth one on the side of your screen," she said.

Simon pressed the video Kerry pointed at and it began to play. The screen was mostly dark, except for the area in the center where the spotlight was shining. The filming captured the whole confrontation that took place between Kerry and Dave Griffins.

"It's the same video, but from a different angle," Simon said.

"But look Simon, it captures a wider view. And the most important part," Kerry said.

Simon paused the video and Kerry rewound it to the beginning. She smiled as she pointed to the bottom of the screen that showed Griffins and his redheaded sidekick sneaking behind the officer keeping back the crowd.

And then captured them crouching under the bright yellow *do not cross* police tape.

CHAPTER 18

I t wasn't as good as watching Dave Griffins' face personally when he heard about the department's countersuit, but hearing from the department's lawyer was pleasure enough. The lawyer informed Kerry that the proof she found on the video should be enough to win the lawsuit or even have it dropped if they were lucky. Kerry wanted a public apology, but the lawyer suggested they not push their luck and just let the case die.

In the end, Kerry knew he was right, and it was better for her to focus her attention on identifying the remains that were found in the mudslide.

Wayne and the forensic crew had gathered all the evidence they were going to be able to find at Crow Island and the whole team was now available to help search the mudslide area for more evidence.

Since the night the mudslide came down, the forensic team was trying to work quickly to search the area in squared-off zones before the next storm hit Lake Pines.

The hill wasn't stable, and the next onslaught of rain risked sending the search team back to square one.

More remains were uncovered but they failed to help advance Kerry's identification of the body. She looked deeper at the damaged neck of the victim and was certain that the cause of death was a broken neck. The bag, clothes and remains all displayed evidence of having been buried which meant it was more than likely murder and not an accidental fall.

The coloring of the bones and decay dated the remains at approximately fifteen years of having been buried, which also was in line with the printing dates on the bills found in the pack. All those years that hikers walked those trails and that cars drove past on the road below without being aware that a murder victim lay buried in the cold, hard ground.

She would have preferred to have had the whole jaw to be able to compare dental records but first, she needed to see how far Wayne got on the missing person's report and tracking down the key.

Kerry found a parking spot in the back lane of the police department and squeezed her Jeep in beside Simon's car. She couldn't wait to tell him that the department's lawyer was hopeful that the new video could help their case and that he even believed they may be able to have the lawsuit dropped altogether. All because he was following her video online.

"Doctor Dearborne," Wayne smiled as Kerry walked into the office.

"Please call me Kerry," she said. "You're starting to make me feel old."

Wayne blushed, "Sorry. Kerry."

"I wanted to come by and see what missing person's reports you were able to dig up from about fifteen years ago," Kerry asked.

"There were thirty-seven," Wayne said.

"That many?" Kerry knew there were a lot of runaways, but she was still shocked to hear it was such a high number.

"I widened my search over five years, but yeah, that many," Wayne said.

"And were you able to narrow down our search to teenage boys?" she asked.

"Sally is a whiz at online searches and all but three have been confirmed either found or deceased. She compiled a list of their names and was going to send it over to you," Wayne said.

"Good. Is there any way she can find out who their doctors were? It would be good to maybe compare some of the minor breaks I noticed on the remains. At least until we can confirm dental records," Kerry said.

"Sure thing."

"And the key?" Kerry asked.

"I have Simon looking into that one," Wayne said.

A smile crossed Kerry's face, it was a good excuse to go sit with him at his desk.

Kerry found Simon organizing pages from his training session into his binder.

"I understand we are working together on this case now," Kerry sat down in the chair next to his desk.

"You mean the key? Yeah," Simon said. "I was able to track down who cut the key. There are only five stores in Lake Pines that have a key cutting machine. When I started asking around, I also found out that at one time each store engraved a specific code into the top rim of the key. It was a trial program that was launched. If a lost key was found it could be turned into the police station and then passed on to the engraver. Then they would be able to contact the owner and return the key."

"Hmm, smart," Kerry said.

"Yeah, the idea was good, but it never took off," Simon said. "But we may have caught a break because this key was cut when this program was in effect."

"Were you able to track down the engraver?" Kerry asked.

"Yes. It was Carver's Hardware on Fifth Street," Simon said. "When I called the store, the teenager working the till had no idea what I was talking about. I'm going back this afternoon to speak with the owner."

"When are you going back?" Kerry asked.

Simon looked at the time, "Now. Want to come along?"

"Why not."

"Good," Simon smiled. "We can talk about naming the dog."

* * *

Mr. Carver was eighty-seven years old and opened the hardware store when he was twenty-one. Since that first day, he stocked, shelved, sold, and served the customers of Lake Pines solely on his own. Last winter he slipped on a patch of ice while shoveling the sidewalk in front of his shop, sending him straight to the hospital for two weeks. His children insisted that he hire a young staff member to help run the store and alleviate most of the physical labor. He fought them, but only slightly. He was ready to relinquish some of the heavy lifting, but before his fall he was too proud to do so.

Joey Miller now spent his days standing behind the counter trying his best to keep Mr. Carver from carrying large boxes and stocking high shelves. Joey tried his best, but Mr. Carver insisted on staying active and doing what he loved. Eventually, they came to an agreement and Mr. Carver began to give Joey more responsibility in the store and Joey, in turn, would not stop Mr. Carver from doing most chores that he loved. As long as he didn't risk getting hurt in the process.

Carver's Hardware still had the same large wood and glass doors that were installed when the shop was first opened. Kerry pulled the large brass handle and the door opened out onto the street and the echo of the small bell that hung on the hinge rang out.

Joey was ringing up a sale of plumbing joints and nodded as Kerry and Simon walked into the store.

Mr. Carver was sitting in the back office and saw them as they entered the store. He smiled and waved them into his office.

"Come in. Sit down," he waved to the chairs across from his desk. "Joey said you needed to trace an old key that I probably engraved."

"Yes sir," Simon handed the small clear plastic bag across the desk.

Mr. Carver pulled his reading glasses from where they were perched on the top of his head and slid them on the edge of his nose.

He mumbled to himself as he read the code that was engraved on the top of the key. He pulled out the bottom drawer of his filing cabinet and fingered through the tabs that were encoded with a series of numbers and letters. A third of the way through the files, he found the code he was looking for and tugged on a yellow tab.

"Here we go," Mr. Carver placed the file on his desk and tilted his head, and looked through the bottom section of his glasses.

He turned over the bag and looked at the keychain that the key was attached to.

"I could have told you who this key belonged to just by the keychain," Mr. Carver said.

"And who would that have been?" Simon asked.

"Sebastian Crow. He had four made for his family. One for him, his wife, and his two kids. Katrina and Kyle."

CHAPTER 19

Kerry went back to her office and Simon returned to the station. Neither of them was aware that Sebastian's son was possibly one of the missing teens. His name wasn't on the list that Sally had compiled, and Simon was returning to the station to have her double-check on the reports that were filed. Now that they had a name, maybe it would be easier to pull up his missing person's report.

Kerry wanted to make sure that she was positive about the remains being Kyle's before she broke the news to Isobella and Katrina. There wasn't an easy way to inform a family member when remains were discovered. Hope was always present, even when there was no contact with a runaway. However, once a body was found, hope ended for that family.

And no matter how frustrating it was dealing with Isobella, she could only imagine how devastating it would be for her to find out her son was confirmed dead the same week she found out her husband had been murdered.

It occurred to Kerry that Isobella leaving Lake Pines and moving to Vancouver also coincided with Kyle's disappearance. It wasn't uncommon for a marriage to break apart after a child died or went missing. She wondered if it was the case for Sebastian and Isobella.

Kerry's phone began to bounce across her desk as it buzzed with the incoming call.

It was from Peter.

"Hi Peter," Kerry answered. "Everything okay with Griffins' lawsuit?"

"Everything seems to be settling with that. Griffins said it must have been a misunderstanding and he, and his employer, are taking a step back from you for a while," Peter said. "But that's not why I'm calling."

"What's up?"

"I got a call from Devon Kozlowski's lawyer yesterday. He said he tried to reach out to you, but you wouldn't take his call," Peter said.

"That's right," Kerry said. "With everything going on with the lawsuit, I decided to stay on my side of the line."

"Probably a good idea considering what he had to say," Peter said.

"Well, don't keep me in suspense. What did he want?"

"He said he had information on the remains that were found in the mudslide," Peter said.

"I think we have a lead on who they belong to. Simon is just confirming some particulars before we say anything," Kerry explained.

"It's more than that Kerry. He said he also knows who killed the kid," Peter said.

"What? Why would he just offer information like that up?" Kerry asked.

"He wanted to make a deal with us concerning the charges in the Sebastian Crow murder he is facing."

"You didn't do it, did you?" Kerry closed her eyes and shook her head.

"If there is a chance to put both of these cases to bed in a short period of time, we need to take it."

"But why? We have Devon's fingerprint at the scene, and he is already in prison. What could he possibly want?" Kerry asked.

"He wanted to be moved to the remand center," Peter said.

"Lower security?" Kerry asked. "He's being charged for murder Peter!"

"He claims his life is in danger where he is. Two inmates attacked him in the cafeteria. He ended up being quite badly beaten and one of the other inmates had an injured neck. The warden wants him gone too," Peter said.

"So, what did Mr. Kozlowski have to say about the remains?" Kerry asked.

Peter didn't answer.

"Peter? What did he say?"

"The remains belong to Kyle Crow," Peter said.

"How can you be sure he's telling the truth?"

"He said he's the one who killed him."

CHAPTER 20

Kerry didn't like it. It was too easy and too clean. In all her years of experience, Kerry learned to be cautious with admissions of guilt. More often than not, it turned out to be a criminal who was lying in order to gain some leniency on a charge.

And that's exactly what was happening with Devon.

Kerry wasn't sure if he would speak to her, but it was worth the try. Wayne was comfortable with accepting Devon's confession and letting Peter pull rank on the case.

Kerry, however, wasn't.

She had a lot of respect for Peter but moving Devon to a lower security prison was just a PR move after the disaster that unfolded with Griffins and the lawsuit. She knew that there was a lot of support for her with the public and now she was trying to bring Sebastian Crow's killer to justice.

The lawsuit didn't change that in her mind.

And Wayne still hadn't gotten around to charging him with the murder of Calvin Crow yet.

Kerry parked in the far end of the parking lot, opting to not park in the spaces reserved for visitors. She wanted to keep her presence at the jail low profile.

The guard on duty signed Kerry in and then called into the holding area for the prisoner to be brought up to the meeting room.

Kerry waited ten minutes before a guard entered the room where she was seated. She was holding Devon's elbow and guiding him to the vacant seat on the opposite side of the table. After he was handcuffed to the table the guard left the room, but only after Kerry insisted that she would be fine. She knew that it was the protocol that each room was monitored by a video camera and that she was safely being watched by the guard on the other side of the two-way mirror.

"So now you want to speak to me," Devon laughed sarcastically.

"Not really. I don't feel like I have any choice since you lied to the arresting officer about having killed Kyle Crow," Kerry goaded Devon with her tone.

It worked.

Devon lunged forward and banged his fists on the table, "I did kill him! How else would I've known it was him on that hill?"

"I think you're just shady enough to know the kind of guys who would have killed Kyle," Kerry said. "It's more likely that you heard them talk about it and you just thought it would be the perfect way to distract everyone from what really happened on Crow Island."

"You're just upset that your boss stepped in and made a deal with me," Devon snapped at her.

"I agree that I'm not happy about that, but I also think there is more to what happened the night that Sebastian Crow was killed than you're telling us. I know someone else was there. Who was it?" Kerry asked.

She hated the idea of another killer roaming free while Devon protected him.

"I don't know what you're talking about," he said.

"I don't believe you could've killed Kyle. Not by yourself anyway. You're too small," she said.

"Well, I did. Ask me anything," Devon challenged her.

"For starters, how did you even know him?" Kerry asked.

"We went to school together."

"Convenient. You went to school together," Kerry mocked him.

"I was fostered with a family in Lake Pines when I was fifteen. I was moved here after my dad bolted and my mom junked out on some drugs. There were no family members who would take me in, so I got thrown into the system and ended up here," he blurted. "I met him when I was forced to enroll at Lake Pines High School."

"Even if that's true, that doesn't prove you killed Kyle," Kerry said. "And if you can't prove any of what you're saying, then the deal you made with the police is off the table."

"We were going to run away. Both of us. He hated living at home and the family I was placed with was threatening to send me away to another family. His sister lived in Toronto and we were going to hop a bus and go out there and stay with her."

"What happened then?" Kerry asked.

"We met up on the hill after school and we had planned to grab the evening bus at the station. We were hiding out on the hill, waiting for most of the traffic to pass and for it to get dark. We didn't want to risk being seen waiting around the bus depot," Devon paused as he remembered back to that night on the hill. "He began to change his mind. Said he didn't want to get dragged back by his parents. He began to get up and leave and I grabbed him by the shoulder and pulled him back. That's when he fell."

"Fell? Where?" Kerry asked.

"He started to pull away after I grabbed his arm and he slipped. His body went shooting back and he hit his head on a rock. I got scared. I didn't know what to do. If I went to get help, there was no way I was going to be able to go home so I just buried him and his bag up there on the hill."

"Where did you get the shovel? I'm assuming you didn't have one in your bag."

"There was a work shed at the foot of the hill that the road construction crew had set up while they were fixing the side of the road. I broke the lock and got a shovel once it was dark. After I buried him and his pack I left. I got the first bus out of the depot and I was gone."

"So, if it was an accident, why not go get help?" Kerry asked. "You wouldn't have been in trouble."

"That's not how things worked out for kids like me," Devon said.

"Why did you come back to Lake Pines?" Kerry finally asked.

Devon paused before he answered, "I was homesick I guess."

Devon gave exact information as to where he buried the body, what Kyle was wearing, what was in his bag along with how Kyle died.

It was enough for Peter to grant him leniency on the Sebastian Crow case and have him moved to another holding facility until his hearing.

The only problem was it was a lie.

CHAPTER 21

Kerry knew that she was walking on thin ice with Peter. The lawsuit was taking its toll on both the murder investigations as well as her reputation. There was a time that she considered leaving Lake Pines and returning to Montreal, but now this was home for her, and she was going to fight to stay.

Devon had no idea that she had been temporarily relieved of her duties as the coroner investigating the Sebastian Crow murder, as well as the remains from the mudslide. Kerry had neglected to tell him that when she visited him in prison. She knew that the absence of truth wasn't necessarily a lie. She just hoped that Peter or Wayne never found out.

Kerry was thinking that Devon might have been on the hill when Kyle was killed and was possibly responsible for his death, but Kyle didn't fall to his death. His neck had been broken and that would have taken more force than a fall from a struggle.

She steered her boat around the channel marker and headed directly for Crow Island. Isobella would still be on the island frantically packing everything up in preparation for the sale and the settling of Sebastian Crow's estate. She asked Wayne to let her be the one to inform Isobella that the remains in the mudslide were possibly Kyle's. Not that she was particularly fond of Isobella, it was just that she didn't think Wayne would have done a great job of speaking with her. He improved somewhat in dealing with grieving family members, but not enough that you would want him breaking that sort of news regularly.

As the boat approached the dock, Isobella could be seen through the front window of the cottage. Her bright fuchsia dress stood in contrast to the faded brown siding and darkened forest to the side of the cottage.

Kerry tied the boat and walked up the steps to the cottage. Isobella folded her hands in the crooks of her elbows when she saw Kerry approach the front door.

"What are you doing here?" Isobella said through the screen door. "I was told you weren't working on Sebastian's case anymore."

"I'm not. But not because I wasn't doing a good job. Just because I have found myself embroiled in a messy lawsuit," Kerry explained. "But I'm not here because of that. Can I please come in and talk to you?"

Isobella relaxed her arms and pushed open the screen door. Kerry thanked her and walked into the cottage. Boxes were piled around the room that was now devoid of paintings, books, and any personal mementos that would have revealed that Sebastian Crow spent most of his life living in these four walls. Kerry noticed that Isobella's eyes were rimmed red and her cheeks were damp with tears.

Opening old wounds when someone close dies is common and something Kerry saw often. It made what she came to Crow Island to say that much harder.

"Can you take a break for a minute so we can talk?" Kerry asked.

"The property inspector is supposed to arrive soon. The new owners want to have the septic field checked out before they sign the final papers on the offer," Isobella said. "I can give you until then."

"Is Katrina here?" Kerry asked.

"No. Why?" Isobella asked.

"She may want to hear what I have to say. I just thought it would be better to hear when you were together and for Katrina to not be alone when she heard," Kerry explained. Trying to soften the blow of the impending news.

"What is it? Sebastian's killer is behind bars. What else could you have to talk to us about?" Isobella was growing impatient and kept looking down at the dock watching for the property inspector to save her from their conversation.

"It doesn't have to do with Sebastian's murder. It has to do with your son," Kerry said. "Kyle."

"Yes, I know who he is," Isobella snapped and then slightly recoiled. "What do you know about him? I haven't seen him since he ran away."

Kerry folded her hands in her lap and gripped her fingers tightly together. "Was that just before you left Lake Pines?"

"Yes. It didn't make any sense trying to stay here with Sebastian. We hadn't been getting along for quite some time and with both of the kids gone, there didn't seem to be much point," Isobella reached for her glass and took a long drink of water.

"Can I ask you why you never filed a missing person's report?" Kerry asked.

She shrugged her shoulders, "There didn't seem to be much sense, really. When Kyle didn't come home from school, I thought he stayed at a friend's house. He did that sometimes on Friday evenings. I called the police when he hadn't come home for dinner by Saturday and they said because of his age that he was probably a runaway. And since –" Isobella's tears forced her words down and she was unable to finish her sentence.

Kerry finished it for her, "Since there were reports of abuse at home, they assumed that he ran away and wasn't missing."

"You know?" Isobella looked shocked.

"I saw the report when I first was investigating Sebastian's murder," Kerry said. "Why didn't you try and find him?"

"Is this why you came here today? To question my parenting skills?"

Kerry closed her eyes and shook her head. "No. I'm sorry. I came because I have news on Kyle."

As if Isobella knew what Kerry was about to say, she bit her lower lip and tears began to form in her eyes.

"I'm sorry Isobella, we believe that Kyle was killed the night he ran away. We found remains in a recent mudslide that points to the possibility that they could be his."

Kerry reached into her pocket and withdrew the key and keychain that she found in the small zippered pocket on his pack.

Isobella's hand shook as she extended her long fingers and held her hand flat. Kerry put the key and keychain on her palm, and Isobella wrapped her fingers around it and pulled it close.

Tears rolled down her face and she cried as she recognized the familiar symbol that all four members of the Crow family had emblazoned on similar key chains. All specially ordered by Sebastian Crow many years ago.

A powerboat pulled up to the dock and a young man jumped out and ran up to the cottage holding a clipboard.

"Give me a minute," Isobella said before she ran from the cottage, wiping her tears as she headed to the dock and then told the property inspector to come back the next day. Then she returned to the cottage where Kerry sat waiting by the window.

"Okay, now you have my full attention," Isobella managed to say through a flood of tears. "I want you to tell me everything you know about what happened to Kyle the night he disappeared."

Kerry looked at Isobella and then steadied herself. Kerry then proceeded to break the news that the man suspected of killing Sebastian is also the same person who admitted to having killed her son fifteen years earlier.

Kerry spent an hour with Isobella after she had started to absorb the news that Kyle was dead and not just gone from Lake Pines. Isobella's tears began to slow and the odd smile appeared as she recalled moments in her son's life that flashed into her memory.

Isobella pulled the family memory book off the shelf above where the games were kept. A faded yellow and white fabric memory book jammed with photographs, drawings, and collages of twigs and bark that were glued to the pages in honor of the hours of exploring that Kyle and Katrina did along the water's shores of Crow Island, folded open and revealed a youth of happiness.

For most of the afternoon, Isobella reminisced about her young family as Kerry patiently listened on, not knowing the people, but fully understanding the emotions.

When it was clear that Isobella was ready for some privacy, Kerry excused herself and left her to revisit the more personal corners of her life. With her husband and son now removed from her life forever, there was much she needed to come to terms with. The first, Isobella said, was to plan an appropriate memorial for them.

The rain had stopped, and the air held the freshness and calmness that Kerry needed.

She started the boat and as she slipped the rope from the knot that held it to the dock her phone buzzed. She pulled it from her pocket as the boat motored out of the bay and read the text from her lawyer.

Dave Griffins has decided to proceed with the lawsuit because he claims to have verifiable evidence that Doctor Kerry Dearborne has displayed unprofessional conduct on more than one occasion, and that in addition to monetary compensation, he is also going to push to have her fired.

Kerry slipped the phone back in her pocket and drove slowly back to town. Preoccupying her mind, wasn't the five million dollars or the threat of losing her job that was bothering her.

Instead, she knew that what happened in Montreal was coming back to haunt her and she needed to be ready.

CHAPTER 22

He had seen the same trick work on television shows and figured he would be able to make it work today. Smuggling cutlery out of the cafeteria was remarkably simple, which was one of the reasons he pushed to get moved here. The difficult part was trying to sharpen the end against the wall in his holding cell. Loudmouthed inmates required the guards to make more frequent trips by the cells throughout the night as they tried to quiet them down with threats of solitary confinement and loss of outdoor privileges. Neither of which seemed to work.

By morning he had to be comfortable with the job he had done on the spoon. After all, he didn't want to kill anyone, he just wanted to do enough harm to start a fight.

Guards were different at every institution that he had been through, and although they had to follow the same procedures, they would often change things up to keep inmates on their toes. The night of constant disruption meant the inmates were given outdoor time before breakfast. A reminder that the guards held control over every small minute of their day.

Ironically, it suited his plan more perfectly.

He already knew who he would target. The short stubby inmate, who was three cells down from his, had made it his job to let everyone know that any, and all, contraband came through him. And only him. Steve had been the longest 'resident' and, as such, he believed that seniority gave him the right of control.

It didn't matter anyhow, he just wanted to start a fight and Steve's ego was just fragile enough that he knew he could goad him into one easily. He wasn't worried about being hurt. With all his years on the streets, he knew that he could take care of himself, and his martial arts training always proved useful when he needed to protect himself against a larger opponent. Today, however, it wasn't about winning. It was about getting out of this jail for good. And this was the first step.

He tucked the sharpened spoon inside his sleeve and folded his wrist back to hold it in place. Knowing that their time outside was limited, he walked directly to the other end of the yard and yelled out Steve's name.

Before Steve had a chance to turn around the spoon was jabbed into his side. Just enough of a stab to make the threat seem real, but shallow enough to elicit a fight response.

He braced himself as Steve's fist came toward his face. He knew it would be only a matter of time before the two lanky guards came running to break up the fight. He could feel the swelling start where Steve's fist landed against his cheekbone and the trickle above his lip told him his nose was probably broken as well. When Steve's foot landed at the base of his ribs he coiled in pain and braced himself for another hit. Soon the guard would separate them, and he would be dragged off. Soon he would be free. He just hoped it would be before anyone knew what really happened with both Sebastian and Calvin Crow.

CHAPTER 23

Focusing on the murder of Calvin Crow was a welcome diversion for Kerry. Even though she doubted she could trust Devon's account for what happened to Kyle Crow, she believed he had something to do with Sebastian Crow's murder. She also didn't think he could have acted alone. He was too small and too frail to be able to take down a man the size of Sebastian. That, and the fact that the police were still unable to find the boots that matched the prints at both murder scenes.

The police were also no closer to figuring out what Sebastian and Calvin were arguing about the day Sebastian was killed. Kerry had a feeling that whatever it was, it connected the two murders together.

The police confirmed the gun used to kill Calvin was registered to him and that the killer must have found it in the cottage the night he was shot. The only prints on the gun were found to be Calvin's and other than the boot print, there was no other evidence.

Although Calvin's business at the boatyard looked like it was in serious trouble, his finances told a different story. His properties had long since been paid off and he held no mortgages or loans with the bank. His investments were healthy and his retirement income well above the standard average. His records showed he was drawing ten thousand dollars a month from his retirement savings even though he only spent less than two.

There was less than two hundred dollars cash in his cottage and it was left untouched by the killer. Typical cottage antiques and collectibles lined shelves and cabinets, but nothing had been removed, broken, or stolen.

Whoever killed Calvin Crow, came to the cottage to do just that.

Sophia pushed open the door to Kerry's office, "Doctor Dearborne, there's a call for you."

"Can you take a message, Sophia?"

"I thought you would want to speak with him," Sophia explained. "It's Nathan Crow, one of Calvin Crow's sons calling trying to find out when his body can be released."

"Thanks, Sophia. I'll take it," Kerry reached for the phone on her desk. "Good morning, Mr. Crow."

"Good morning, Doctor Dearborne."

"I'm so sorry for your loss," Kerry began. "I can only imagine what you and your brother must be going through."

"Thank you, it was quite a shock to get that call," Nathan said. "I was calling because my brother and I want to finalize the arrangements for our father's funeral soon."

"I understand. I can contact the funeral home and let them know they are free to begin their services if you like?" There was only one funeral home in Lake Pines, so there was no need to ask which one they were using.

"I would appreciate that, Doctor Dearborne."

"We do have a forensic team at your father's cottage still, however, they should be able to complete their work by the end of tomorrow," Kerry said.

"Thank you," Nathan said. "My brother and I will be coming into Lake Pines in a few days to settle his estate as well."

Kerry then asked the difficult question, "Do you or your brother remember a man by the name of Devon Kozlowski? He is about your age."

"No. Is that the man who killed my father?" Nathan asked.

"We believe so," Kerry said. "He is also accused of killing your uncle Sebastian. If we can make a connection between the two murders, we can then charge him with your father's shooting."

"I'll ask my brother, but we all hung out with the same kids, so I doubt he'll know him either."

"He apparently was a friend of your cousin Kyle's."

"I didn't really know a lot of his friends or who he hung out with," Nathan said.

"Were you not close with your cousin growing up?" Kerry asked.

"When we were really small, we were, but my mom didn't want us hanging around them as we grew older."

"Why was that?" Kerry asked.

"She thought it was an angry house," Nathan explained with a light chuckle. "At least that's how she described it. She would say '*I get a bad vibe when I'm there*' and then that was that."

Kerry thanked Nathan and then once again offered her condolences on his loss.

"Thank you Doctor Dearborne. My dad was a great guy. He was always thinking of other people, and he didn't deserve to die the way he did. I hope you can find his killer for certain and make sure he's locked up for good."

"That's what we are aiming for, Mr. Crow."

Kerry ended the call and with renewed vigor, she decided to head out to the island where Calvin was murdered. She needed to find proof of Calvin's killer, no matter what Peter said about her partial suspension.

She grabbed her keys and headed out the door. Sophia could manage the reports and it would keep her busy for the rest of day, and she wanted to see what she could find out about Calvin's killer.

* * *

There were only two officers on the island continuing their search when Kerry arrived. The ground was still damp from the two days of rain and the air was chilled from the previous night's drop in temperature.

A gentle breeze picked up from the bay and as the branches gave way to their force, remnants of the rain that remained on the leaves landed on Kerry's head as she walked up from the dock.

Kerry nodded to the officer who was taking the last of his photos as she walked into the cottage.

"I'm just finishing up in here, it's all yours," the young officer turned around and took three more photos before leaving the cottage.

The cottage was small and the layout simple. Bedrooms and bathroom to the left, a large living room in the center, and then two extra rooms on the right.

Kerry entered the first room on the right and noticed it had been designated as an office. It was old and dusty, but cleaner and more organized than the boatyard was.

Kerry found the files that contained Calvin's banking and investment information and like the police reports found, they were both in good shape. She also found an additional handwritten ledger that showed sums of money that were deposited to another account over the course of several years. There was no reference other than the account number, dates, and amounts. She would bring the whole file to Wayne and he could have someone track down the owner of the account. It may be nothing, but it was worth looking into.

Other files contained information relevant to the boating industry and mechanics magazine clippings. She quickly flipped through those but found nothing of interest to the case.

She grabbed the last file in the cabinet that was marked 'Crow Cottages'.

Inside were plans and layouts of both Sebastian's and Calvin's cottages. Faded black and white photographs tumbled onto the floor.

Kerry bent down to grab them. Various pictures of the brothers in their youth showed a close and warm relationship. Images of their camping trips, family barbeques, and even shots of them both building

Calvin's cottage. Kerry stopped when she reached a photo of the half–completed building site.

A photo of the inside of Calvin's cottage caught her attention. The photo showed both men standing in the area that was just outside the room where she sat now.

Kerry pushed back the chair she was sitting in and rushed into the hall. She bent down and pulled back the carpet and saw what the two young men in the photo were laughing at.

She reached down and lifted the panel in the floor and revealed a trapdoor that opened to the underside of the cottage.

CHAPTER 24

Memorials were strange events. The intent was to gather to remember the lives of people who had died. But in fact, memorials were fashioned more for the people left behind. There were various reasons for family members to hold memorials. Some felt a deep sense of loss and weren't ready to let go and it was their way of hanging on.

Some, as Kerry saw too many times, were held for the benefit of appearances. Families that were expected to act a certain way while in public and for the consumption of other people's satisfaction.

Guilt was more the reason Kerry believed that most memorials were held after someone died. Guilt for not being more present while the person was still alive. Guilt for their pride in having taken a hard stance in an argument at the expense of a life lost in friendship and love.

Kerry couldn't quite decide what the reasons were that Isobella and Katrina were holding a memorial. They had three family members they were going to need to bury in the next week, but none of which they really kept in touch with.

Isobella let Katrina choose the location for their memorial since it would just be the two of them present. Katrina designated an area on Crow Island where she and her father would sit and watch the sunset together.

It was how she wanted to remember both he and her brother.

It was on the far side of the island where it would be next to impossible to build anything. She thought the rocky outcrop and the steep cliff edge that hung over the water would make it a sure bet that it would be safe from construction and could remain untouched. That way she could be content with the knowledge that their resting place would remain untouched, no matter who the owner ended up being.

Isobella had already asked that the remains of her father and brother be cremated so she could spread them on a designated spot where they could be close to the place they loved the most.

Since they had to wait for the investigations to be complete before any of the remains could be released,

Katrina and Isobella were in the process of preparing the area for the upcoming planned memorial.

Isobella was 'cleansing' the area so that only peaceful spirits would exist there. Katrina was clearing debris from the rocks where she was going to have a stone plaque carved and set into the ground.

Kerry thought that as fractured as the Crow family was, that the two remaining members deserved some emotional support and maybe this tragedy could bring Isobella and Katrina close again.

"Doctor Dearborne?" Isobella was surprised when she saw Kerry standing quietly beside a tree. "I didn't know you were coming."

"I wanted to show my support. I think it's important to do what we can to remember the lives of those that we loved and are now gone. Especially when they are taken so violently."

Isobella rested her hand on Kerry's shoulder, "I agree. That's why we are preparing the area to clear the spirits and make sure that Sebastian and Kyle can rest peacefully."

Kerry watched for the next twenty minutes while the mother and daughter worked quietly assembling rocks and deciding where the best place would be to finally lay the carved stone when it was completed.

When they were done Katrina folded the blanket she had laid on the ground and headed back to the cottage.

Kerry walked back with Isobella, letting Katrina walk ahead.

"Isobella, this may not be the best time, but I need to ask you a question?" Kerry said.

"I'm not sure if I have an answer, but ask away," Isobella said.

"Do you have any idea who Calvin would have been sending money to over the last number of years? We found entries in his ledger of payments to an account but neither of his kids knew about it and I was just wondering if you could shed any light on it. It may be nothing, but I'm hoping it can establish a link to why Devon killed both Sebastian and Calvin."

"Why would you think that?" Isobella asked.

"They were overheard arguing the day that Sebastian was killed, and it seemed like an incredible coincidence."

Isobella shrugged her shoulders, "Sorry, I don't have an answer for you."

They reached the cottage and Isobella excused herself, "I'm sorry but today has been really draining. I'm going to go to bed early tonight," Isobella walked up the steps and opened the door to the cottage, and then turned around. "Oh, and Doctor Dearborne, thanks for coming by today."

Kerry nodded and began to walk toward her boat. As she was untying the boat's rope from the cleat, she thought about heading back up to the cottage to ask Katrina why she had called her. Then as the lights to the porch were turned off, she decided that tonight was not the right time.

She would call Katrina tomorrow and find out what she wanted.

CHAPTER 25

A thud hid the door and sent the puppy into an excited frenzy as he barked at the unseen threat outside the front door. Kerry jumped at the sound of his high-pitched barking and her hand flicked in reaction to the sound, spilling hot coffee over the front of her pajamas.

"It's just the paper!" Kerry shouted, knowing her explanation meant nothing to the eager pup.

Kerry lowered her cup to the table, grabbed a tea towel, and dabbed the coffee from her pajamas, table, and arm. She padded toward the front door, the pup nipping at her heels as she walked. She opened the door and the morning paper tumbled inside.

"See," Kerry said to the pup. "There's your attacker."

She reached down and scooped up the paper before closing the door and returning to what was left of her morning coffee.

Completely disinterested with the paper, the pup rambled off and dove headfirst into its earlier battle with the stuffed hedgehog Simon bought him the previous day, leaving Kerry to finish her breakfast in peace.

She wasn't too far into the news when the heading stretched across the article on the top of the third page caught her eye.

"Child Abuser Finds Friend In Coroner's Defence"

Kerry gleaned the story but was able to get the gist of it from the headline's perfectly worded hook. Along with the implication that she was protecting a child abuser and keeping the press from covering the story. Article courtesy of Dave Griffins and fear-mongering courtesy of Laura Martin. She folded the paper closed and poured her coffee down the sink.

She knew that the best way to forget about Dave Griffins and the stinging memory from Montreal was to focus on the bodies she had waiting for her in her lab.

At least by giving the dead some peace, maybe she could find some herself.

* * *

Peter was sitting at Wayne's desk when Kerry walked into the police station. The case files on the three bodies that were in Kerry's lab were laid out in front of him and Wayne was doing his best to summarize their findings.

Peter sat patiently nodding as Wayne stammered on recounting every finding since they first were called about Sebastian Crow. Peter saw Kerry approaching the desk and waved her over as Wayne was talking.

"How are you holding up?" Peter asked.

"You mean since you banned me from working on Sebastian's case?" Kerry said.

"You were not banned. You were just asked to step back until the case with Dave Griffins is settled. Any work in your lab is fine, you know that Kerry," Peter said.

"I know. Sorry for snapping," Kerry apologized. "I don't see how my being kept from the murder scenes makes any sense."

"It should be a moot point after today. If we're lucky," Wayne added.

Kerry looked at both Peter and Wayne, "What are you talking about?"

"Your court case is today," Peter said. "You didn't forget, did you?"

Kerry looked at her watch and quickly turned and ran out of the police station. She arrived at the courthouse and ran up the stairs just as the police department's lawyer was dialing her number.

"Where were you?" he asked. "It's kind of important that you be here today."

"Sorry, I forgot," Kerry said, and walked past him and through the front doors. Hoping that would be the end of any lecture.

William Turnbull was the department's lawyer and a third-generation Lake Pines resident. His family settled in the area before many cottagers even knew about that area of the country. Working both in the small town and in neighboring districts, William was able to sustain a healthy practice and continue living in the small town of Lake Pines which he grew to love. His work for the police department mainly consisted of complaints from the public and press, much like the one he was working on for Kerry today.

Their steps echoed in the marble hallway as they walked with rushed steps to the courtroom.

"Griffins won't have much of a leg to stand on. His main argument is that there was no indication that the area he was in was off-limits," William said as he pulled open the door to the small courtroom where the hearing was being held.

"You know that's not the truth," Kerry said in response.

William put his hand, palm facing Kerry, "Relax, just let me do my job. You just sit there and look doctorly. Today is not the day to be antagonistic."

They took their seats at their designated table and Dave Griffins shot Kerry a sneer as he sat beside his lawyer and the owner of the Lake Pines Daily News.

"He is so smug," Kerry whispered to William.

Everyone in the courtroom was silenced by the arrival of the judge. After the standard introduction, announcements, and the reading of the charges, the lawyers went to work defending their clients.

The paper's team had an organized strategy, attacking every interaction that Kerry had with Dave Griffins over the last few months.

"It's like he planned this lawsuit," Kerry mumbled so only her lawyer could hear.

The judge lowered her glasses and asked the plaintiff's lawyers, "Do you have any more witnesses, Counsellor?"

"Yes, your honor. We would like to call Doctor Kerry Dearborne to the stand," the lawyer tucked his right hand into his pocket and glanced toward the defense table.

Kerry slid her chair back and began to walk toward the stand. She could feel the sting of Dave Griffins' eyes watch her as she took her seat in the witness box but refused to make eye contact with him.

Kerry was sworn in, promised to tell the truth, and nothing but and then folded her hands on her lap and waited.

And then it came.

No dance of a hundred questions. No preamble to her incompetence. Just the one question she was hoping wouldn't come.

"Doctor Dearborne, can you tell us about your investigation into the death of Mr. Paul Jenkins?"

And there it was. Montreal had come back to haunt her.

CHAPTER 26

Kerry looked forward, only making eye contact with the lawyer asking her questions. She knew if she glanced at Dave Griffins, even for a short moment, that her anger would swell. And if she took the time to glance at her lawyer, she would have seen the look of shock and anger on William Turnbull's face.

Kerry had never told him about the case in Montreal because she didn't think it had any bearing on the ludicrous case that Dave Griffins launched against her. That was what they were defending today.

She hadn't even told Simon about what happened, and Peter only knew because she wanted to be completely honest about why she left a lucrative career in Montreal. In fact, it was a memory that she would rather erase, but that's not how life works.

Kerry straightened her shoulders and opened her mouth to speak with her lawyer had managed to compose himself and stand, "Relevance, your honor?"

The judge turned to Dave Griffins' lawyer, perched in front of the witness box, and asked him why the case of Mr. Paul Jenkins was relevant to the current lawsuit.

"Your honor, how Doctor Dearborne approached the murder investigation of Mr. Jenkins speaks to her moral compass."

Anger flushed Kerry's face and she pressed her lips together, forcing down a flurry of harsh words she knew would instinctively come. She shot a glance at her lawyer, imploring him to speak.

She didn't need to. William bolted up from his seat, "Your honor, this is turning into a defamation onslaught, with the only purpose of slandering a credible and professional Doctor who not only is a highly skilled coroner who has helped with hundreds of investigations, but she is also a respected member of our Lake Pines community," looking directly at Dave Griffins when he spoke the words 'respected member of our Lake Pines community'.

Kerry couldn't help but smile at the silent jab toward Dave Griffins. Score one for William Turnbull.

"Counsellor, I have to agree with Mr. Turnbull. Unless you can justify your line of questioning, I'll have to ask you to move along," the judge slid her glasses back on her face.

"Your honor, there is a direct resemblance between Sebastian Crow and Paul Jenkins, and I think we can draw proof that the way the two cases are handled is because of that similarity."

The judge contemplated the argument and then allowed the line of questioning with a warning, "But don't take it too far."

Kerry was prepared for the question and after William's staunch defense and jab at Dave Griffins, she was prepared to face it head-on.

"Doctor Dearborne, do you need me to repeat the question?"

Kerry shook her head, "No. Paul Jenkins had been found stabbed in his home. At first glance, it appeared that he had interrupted a robbery in his home and was attacked defending himself."

"That's not what happened, was it, Doctor Dearborne?"

"No, it wasn't."

"Skip ahead to the actual reason Paul Jenkins was attacked and killed, will you?"

"It was a coordinated attack by three people who lived in his town and they each worked together to cover it up. But the police eventually found proof of who was responsible."

"And, you helped with that investigation, did you not?"

"Yes. That was part of my job," Kerry explained.

"There was mounting public opposition to the number of resources that were spent on the investigation into the death of Paul Jenkins, was there not?"

"It was a murder. And yes, there was."

"And were you specifically asked to step back from this investigation?"

"I received threatening phone calls if that's what you mean."

"And what was the relationship of these three individuals to Paul Jenkins"

"He was their children's hockey coach."

"And why was he targeted and eventually killed by these individuals?"

"They felt that their children had not received justice and that Mr. Jenkins had deserved to be punished."

"Why did their children need to find justice?"

"He was accused of hitting the children during practice. He apparently used heavy-handed tactics when he thought kids weren't pulling their weight. Was it wrong? Yes. But, murdering someone is wrong, even if-" then Kerry stopped speaking, catching herself before she uttered the final words.

But it was too late, Dave Griffins' lawyer spoke them for her, "Even if the man was a monster." He then turned to the judge, "That's all your honor."

CHAPTER 27

By the time it was William's turn, instead of calling Kerry to the stand, he called Dave Griffins first, changing his strategy. She was relieved and took the opportunity to try and compose herself as she sat in her seat and listened. Hoping that her lawyer had a plan of attack greater than Dave Griffins' lawyer did.

When his name was called, he shifted his seat back, slowly stood and buttoned his jacket, and then walked toward the witness stand to take his seat. He deliberately walked close to where Kerry was sitting and mouthed the words 'you'll be sorry' as he made his way to the stand.

Kerry wrapped her fingers together and held her hands flat on her lap so no one could see the fist she was squeezing with them.

"Mr. Griffins, what do you do at the Lake Pines Daily News?"

"I'm a reporter."

"Are you assigned to a specific area of the news to focus on?"

"No. Lake Pines is a very small operation, so whatever news seems relevant is the news that we are told to focus on?"

"We, being the reporters?"

"Yes."

"And it's your editor, Mr. Graves who tells you what to report on?"

"Not specifically. He leaves it up to our discretion."

"So, it's your decision to follow the stories that you believe are of top priority to the residents of Lake Pines?"

"Yes."

"And you only focus on stories that are of top priority to the residents of Lake Pines?"

"That's right. That's why I was trying to report on the unsolved murder of one of our oldest residents."

Dave sat back in the witness booth, looking more relaxed than Kerry had hoped he would at this point.

"So, you believe safety is of great importance to the residents in the area?"

"Yes, of course."

"And, I would assume, the health of the residents is important?"

"Yes."

"Mr. Griffins, did you receive a call from Mrs. Peterson on June 29th?"

"I don't know. Maybe. Um, I think so."

"Well, did you, or didn't you?"

Dave looked over at his lawyer and boss and they both nodded at him. A sign to answer the question. Dave then took a deep breath and faced Kerry's lawyer.

"Yes, I did."

"And what exactly was Mrs. Peterson calling you about Mr. Griffins?"

"She thought there was an issue with the town's water."

"She more than thought, Mr. Griffins, she knew."

William handed a sheet to both the judge and Dave Griffin's lawyer, "This is the information that Mrs. Peterson had forwarded to Mr. Griffins on that day and had called him about three times previously. However, Mr. Griffins refused to report on this issue, even with the documented information she had collected."

"I object, your honor," Dave's lawyer shouted. "Relevance?"

"Sustained. How does this relate to this case Mr. Turnbull?" the judge asked.

"It demonstrates that on several occasions Mr. Griffins has pushed aside less glamourous stories to focus on, and harass, my client. As she investigated serious cases, Mr. Griffins' interference risked tainting evidence of those cases," William responded.

"I'll allow it," the judge determined.

"So, I will ask you again, Mr. Griffins, why did you refuse to ignore information from Mrs. Peterson?"

Dave hesitated then finally said, "I didn't think it was newsworthy."

"Like snapping a gruesome picture of a murder victim would be?"

"Argumentative," Dave's lawyer snapped.

"I agree. Keep it respectful Mr. Turnbull," the judge warned.

"Sorry your honor," William apologized but his point was made. He grabbed a piece of paper from the bottom of his folder. "Mr. Griffins, how long have you been a reporter at the Lake Pines Daily News?"

"About seven years."

"Closer to eight, actually," William corrected Dave.

"Sure, okay."

"Have you considered leaving the employ of the Lake Pines Daily News at any point during that time?"

Dave nervously glanced at his editor who was sitting next to his lawyer.

"Mr. Griffins, would you like me to rephrase the question?"

"No. I, uh, yeah. Once or twice applied to a few other companies."

"Was one of those companies one with national distribution?"

Dave sat quietly and a red blush rose to his face.

"Answer the question, Mr. Griffins," the judge instructed.

"Yes, it was."

"Did you get the job, Mr. Griffins?"

"No."

"Why was that?"

"They said I needed to have more serious cases on my portfolio."

"Like a murder investigation Mr. Griffins?"

"Yes."

After Dave muttered his answer in court, Kerry's lawyer presented further documentation proving that he had pushed aside cases that he deemed boring in favor of tracking down stories he could embellish with hype for his portfolio.

That, along with the video proving that he trespassed into an area cordoned off by the police, the judge had no choice but to rule in Kerry's favor and toss Dave Griffins' lawsuit out of court.

Kerry couldn't help but smile as the case came to a swift end and her lawyer told her she was done with the lawsuit.

"The paperwork will all be handled between lawyers from this point on Doctor Dearborne," William told her. "You're free to go. Just a word of advice. It would still be a good idea to avoid Dave Griffins for a while."

"Where did you get that information on him?" Kerry asked.

"Turns out," William whispered. "Many of his colleagues feel the same way about him that you do."

She quickly thanked her lawyer, and before the editor of the Lake Pines Daily News had a chance to speak with her, she ran from the courtroom and headed directly to her car.

She started her car and put it into drive as she pulled her phone from her pocket.

She wanted to go out to Crow Island and check on the possibility of the trap door. It was all she could think of during the trial. She couldn't remember if the forensic team looked underneath the cottage. If the killer was aware of the trap door, it would make the ideal entry into the cottage without being traced.

Wayne's number rang three times before going to voice mail. Kerry began to speak but not wanting to leave a rambling message, she decided to end the call and try again later.

Hopefully, by the time she called Wayne, she would have the proof they needed to find the killer responsible for Sebastian's murder. And maybe even link it to Calvin's shooting.

Kerry approached the exit for the courthouse parking lot and waited while two emergency police cars rushed past her with their lights and sirens blaring.

Kerry wanted to focus on what she would say to Isobella when she arrived on Crow Island and how she was going to explain what she was looking for.

She rolled up her window and turned up the radio to block out the sound of the sirens.

CHAPTER 28

Gray clouds hung low in the sky and threatened more rain on the area. The ground was already slick with dampness and the ground was near the point of saturation. Kerry slipped her raincoat overtop of her shirt and switched out her shoes.

If she was going to crawl around under Sebastian Crow's cottage, she was going to need a more sensible pair of shoes. She drove her boat from the main dock with the roof on in hopes that if it did start to pour that she would be protected.

The breeze picked up by the time Kerry reached the island. Ropes were blowing loose from the bow of her boat and were bouncing against the water's surface spraying water on the windshield.

The dock was devoid of activity, but she could see Isobella's boat parked inside the boathouse. Kerry pulled alongside the edge of the dock that was nearest the steps to the cottage and secured her boat.

Small red markers were stuck in the ground on thin metal rods. Their plastic flags were being blown by the wind and the wire bent to the point the top almost touched the ground. Surveyors markings, Kerry knew, for a new cottage that was sure to be built by the next owners once they took possession.

Kerry wondered how Katrina felt about the sale or if she felt it was a necessary closure to the pain she would have suffered as a child. After all, she never returned to Lake Pines after she moved to Toronto.

Isobella said that she planned to return to Vancouver once Sebastian's estate was settled. However, with Kyle's remains being found, Isobella wanted to also see that he had a proper funeral alongside his father.

A large box sat on the front step marked 'donation'. Kerry walked around the box on her way to the front door and glanced inside. Board games, cards, and fishing gear were packed neatly inside. Aged but full of memories, the contents of the box seemed oddly placed next to the Louis Vuitton bag that held Isobella's clothes.

"Doctor Dearborne, I didn't know you were coming by?" Isobella walked out the front door with two more items to add to the nearly full donation box. She placed them neatly inside and then brushed her hands together, removing any dust or emotional attachment to the items.

"I didn't want to intrude. I just wanted to check something else," Kerry said.

Isobella surprised Kerry with a small smile and raised a hand toward the door, "Why don't you come in and tell me what it is you're looking for."

The two women stepped inside the cottage. Most of Sebastian's belongings had been packed away and Kerry wondered how many would be saved and how many would be thrown out or donated.

It was such a sad way for a lifetime of attachments and memories to end up.

"I was at Calvin's cottage investigating his shooting when I came across some old photos of both he and Sebastian," Kerry said.

She pulled out the pictures and handed them to Isobella. Isobella reached out and took the photographs from Kerry's grasp. A warm smile passed over her face as she looked back at the two brothers in their youth.

"They were inseparable as kids. Did you know when Sebastian decided to move to Lake Pines permanently, Calvin followed him here and opened the boatyard?" Isobella said. "Wow, this was such a long time ago. A lifetime really."

"Were all of you close?" Kerry asked.

Isobella nodded, "Our kids were the same age and grew up together. Although, Calvin's boys didn't grow distant from him."

Kerry, not sure what to say, just quietly listened as Isobella spoke.

"They both moved to Thunder Bay to go to school and they never left," Kerry sensed that Isobella was thinking about the distant relationship she and Sebastian had with their children.

Kerry changed the topic when she realized that Isobella was getting sad.

"I was interested in this one picture, in particular. The one where they are building Calvin's cottage," Kerry pointed to the photograph she was talking about.

Isobella chuckled, "I remember that day! The kids got so sunburned. They refused to stay out of the water because it was so hot outside. Oh, well . . . what was it about the picture that brought you here?"

"There's a trap door in the floor at Calvin's cottage. Is there one here in this cottage?" Kerry asked.

"Oh, yes! Sebastian put them in most of the cottages he worked on. It was difficult for him to fit into tight spaces, you know, because he was a larger man. And since his job often required him to be underneath cottages, he devised these trap doors in the floors of the cottages he worked on so he could get underneath easily." Isobella walked to the hall at the back of the cottage and turned on the light. "He convinced his dad to let him install this one when he was a teenager. It was the first one he built."

"Who knew this trap door was here?" Kerry asked.

"A lot of people. Sebastian would brag about it to anyone who was over. Plus, he put them in most of the cottages he did plumbing work in," Isobella crossed her arms. "Why?"

Kerry pulled a pair of gloves out of her pocket and snapped them over her hands, "Has anyone opened this since Sebastian was killed?"

"No. I don't think so," Isobella said. "I don't know why anyone would."

Kerry slid her finger in the small hole that was disguised as a knot in the floorboard and pulled it up.

Immediately the scent of damp mustiness wafted toward her face and she coughed at the stench it released into the room. In addition to the dampness that naturally built up underneath the cottage, it wasn't uncommon for muskrats and rodents to take shelter in such areas. Creating a stench-filled area where they ate, bred, and died.

Isobella stepped back and covered her nose with the sleeve of her sweater.

Kerry folded the trap door completely open until it lay on the floor of the hall revealing the crawl space below the cottage. She had a clear and unobstructed view of the ground below.

She let out a sigh of relief and release from the frustration she was feeling with the murder investigation as she glanced down at the area under the cottage that had been hidden by the hatch.

Bloody handprints stained the boards and next to a completely clear and untouched set of boot prints was a hunting knife. And it was stained with Sebastian Crow's dried blood.

CHAPTER 29

O fficer Jimmy Peterson was disabled with a short, fast jab to his neck. The last thing he said he remembered was seeing the headline in the sports section of the newspaper before his eyes became blurry and he started to fall sideways. By the time the nurse found him on the floor, Devon had stolen the young officer's keys and was driving away from the hospital.

Peterson was a recent recruit to the Lake Pines Police Department or LPPD which is how he would proudly refer to his new employer and was eager to impress his superiors with his skills and abilities. He was chosen to guard Devon's hospital room, not because of his keen policing skills that he was so enthusiastic to display to his superiors, but because he was six foot two, two hundred and twenty pounds and had a chance of restraining any prisoner who intended on escaping.

This, however, proved to be flawed thinking. As the nurse was tending to the cuts on the side of Peterson's head, he just kept murmuring that this was going to blow his chance at getting a decent posting for a while.

Soon, as if prompted by Peterson's murmurs, Wayne pounded down the hospital hallway, his boots reverberating each angry step across the linoleum floor. His steps echoed his intended direction ahead of his arrival and Peterson shooed the nurse's hand from his head as he stood to greet his boss as he turned the corner.

"Sir, I don't know what happened," Peterson stammered apologetically.

Wayne shook his head and waved his hand down, "Sit down, Officer. You look like you've been beaten across the side of your head with a bat."

Jimmy raised his hand and patted the side of his head and felt the sticky mass of hair that his boss was referring to.

"It's not a big cut, sir. It just bled a lot," he explained. "I can still help in the search."

"I have Simon co-ordinating a search right now. Shouldn't be too hard, since the suspect *does* have your car," Wayne snapped. "Why don't you start from the beginning and tell me everything."

"The prisoner was transported from the jail because of the injuries he sustained in a fight. He was treated in the emergency room and I was called in to guard him in his room," Jimmy reddened as he spoke the last few words, knowing he failed in his one given duty of guarding the prisoner.

"You *do* know he is a murder suspect, don't you?" Wayne asked.

Jimmy nodded, "Yes sir. He was restrained to the bed and the only people allowed in or out of his room were hospital staff."

"Was there anyone you didn't recognize hanging around the hall or trying to get into his room?" Wayne asked.

"No, just the staff of the hospital sir," Jimmy answered.

"Do you remember exactly who went into his room?" Wayne prodded.

"There was the doctor who operated on him. I think his name was Doctor Desmond Jones. Then there were the three nurses. The shorter nurse in the pink scrubs with flowers printed all over them. She is sitting at the nursing station now. The nurse with the dark hair and plain blue scrubs and then the one who was cleaning up my head just before you arrived," Jimmy pointed to the clipboard hanging on the wall next to the hospital room door. "I had them all sign in as per regulations."

Wayne stepped closer to where the clipboard hung and removed it from the nail it dangled from. He ran his finger down the few entries that were noted and the officer was right. There were seven visits by four hospital staff, and each one signed in as Peterson said.

Wayne glanced across the hall to the nurses' station and then down the hall to where two nurses stood next to the medicine cart discussing a patient's file.

"Officer? What did you say the second nurse was wearing?" Wayne asked.

"Plain blue scrubs, sir," Peterson recalled.

"Like the ones the doctors wear?" Wayne clarified.

"Yeah, exactly like those," Peterson said.

Wayne took in the variety of patterns and colors worn by the nurses and as he glanced at the flowers, polka dots, and puppies printed on the material he realized he didn't see one plain blue nursing uniform.

Wayne shook his head and turned around and hurried down the hall, "Come on officer, we need to find out if this hospital has a security camera. And if it does, you need to point out the nurse in the plain blue uniform."

CHAPTER 30

Simon was pleased with the fact that both Wayne and Peter had enough confidence in his abilities to put him in charge of coordinating the search efforts for an escaped prisoner, however, he couldn't help but wish that he was out on the streets searching for Devon himself. Instead, he was at his desk tracking the efforts of the few officers they had available to conduct a street search. Since he was not just any missing prisoner, Simon was authorized to pull officers from other duties to participate in the search.

Devon was a viable suspect in two recent murder investigations and possibly numerous thefts. There was no accounting for how aggressive he could be if he felt he was being threatened. The tracking device for Officer Peterson's police cruiser had been disabled and they lost track of it somewhere close to Blackburn Road on the east side of town. Simon sent most of the officers in that direction and had half of them begin a door-to-door search and the other half were instructed to search abandoned cabins and buildings in the area.

In addition to closing the roads out of town, Simon was hopeful that his request for a helicopter search of the area would be approved. The dense forest that Lake Pines was famous for, also risked hindering the search for their escaped prisoner.

Simon was standing in front of his search map, marking off the areas and buildings that had already been combed by the officers. He shaded each area with a red mark and was determining where to send the next crew of officers when his phone rang.

"Officer Phillips," Simon answered his phone without moving his eyes from the map.

"Simon, it's me," Wayne spoke into the phone quickly. "Any news on the search?"

"Not yet. How is Peterson?" Simon asked.

"Looks worse for wear than he actually is. I suspect his ego is quite bruised too," Wayne said. "Look, it seems as if there was a woman who posed as a nurse who entered Devon's room. She may be responsible for helping break him out of his room."

"Any idea of who she is?" Simon asked.

"There seems to be some problem with the security camera at the hospital," Wayne turned his back from the two security guards who were fumbling with the keyboard trying to find the images that Wayne was looking for. "Turns out no one is quite sure who has the master code that is needed to access the film. I'll give them a few more minutes before contacting the head administrator. Until then I want you to do something."

"Sure thing," Simon said.

"If this woman posed as a nurse to get into Devon's room, there is a good chance she may have visited him at the jail. And I have a feeling that their security system is slightly more reliable," Wayne said just loud enough for the two security guards and Officer Peterson to hear. "Call over and see if Devon had any visitors and if so, find out who they were."

"I'll get on that right now," Simon ended the call and a few seconds later the line for the prison security office was ringing.

A familiar voice answered the line and Simon brought Lisa up to speed on both Devon's escape from the hospital and what he was hoping she could find in their records. Lisa grew up next door to Simon and was his sister's best friend since they were five. Lisa was a spunky woman with cropped blonde hair and is what his father would refer to as 'a real pistol' when they were growing up. She would frequently be responsible for setting pranks and jokes on her friends, constantly setting the mood for a fun evening. Lisa was the swizzle stick in his sister's large group of friends, and she was also the reason his ultra-shy sister had a social life in her teens. But at work, Lisa was completely professional, and Simon knew that he could count on her to locate the woman they were looking for if, in fact, she visited Devon while he was in the prison. Lisa listened to Simon and he could tell with her frequent 'uh-huhs' that she was writing down the information as he spoke.

"Give me a sec," Lisa said and put Simon on hold. A few moments later she was back on the line and flipping through the visitor's log. "Looks like there were mostly repeat visitors. You and Wayne, of course. His lawyer and Doctor Dearborne were both here just before he was moved," Lisa said as she read out loud the names of the visitors from the log. "Hmm. There is one other person who visited him as well."

"When was that?" Simon asked.

"Two days before he was transferred to the hospital because of the fight," Lisa explained. Simon could hear the paper rustling through the phone.

Simon had hoped that his accomplice would eventually show up at the prison, now maybe they could figure out who he was. "What was his name?" Simon asked, poised ready to write the name down.

"It was a woman," Lisa corrected him, "and her name is Katrina Crow."

CHAPTER 31

Wayne tossed his hat on top of his seat as he passed by Sally. He headed directly toward Simon and slammed his hands on the desk. Wayne tried to show he was calm and in charge, but having two murder cases, seemingly connected, sitting on his books unsolved, was taking a huge toll on his patience.

"Do we have any idea why the daughter of the man that Devon was accused of killing was visiting him just days before he managed to escape our custody?" Wayne yelled.

Simon leaned back in his chair, completely unfazed by Wayne's bravado, "No idea Wayne," Simon answered. "Best guess would be she was curious about the man who was being charged with killing her father. Remember, she didn't seem to hold the same bitterness that Isobella does against Sebastian. She was pretty shaken up over his death."

"Well, she also matches the description of the unknown nurse who was in Devon's room just before Peterson was knocked out," Wayne said.

"No!" Simon exclaimed.

Wayne straightened himself and folded his arms across his chest, "and even though the hospital video was grainy you could still tell it was Katrina."

"But, then that means. . ." Simon began.

"That Katrina and the killer knew each other," Wayne finished.

* * *

Kerry arrived at the station just as Wayne and Simon were deciding who should be the one to warn Isobella that not only had Devon escaped, but that Katrina may be involved.

"You don't want to jump to any conclusions," Kerry cautioned them both, "you know how these things have a way of turning out."

Wayne held up both of his hands, palms facing out, "I know, but we can't ignore the facts. Devon has been charged with Sebastian Crow's murder. We are also pretty sure he is responsible for the murder of Sebastian's brother Calvin, and, he also admitted to killing Kyle."

"We still aren't sure if Devon admitted to killing Kyle just to try and bargain his way into another facility," Kerry said.

"He knew exactly what was in the bag Kerry," Simon said, "and, he told us the body and bag were Kyle's before we even told Isobella."

"I guess," Kerry said. "It's just too neat."

Wayne and Simon both agreed, "But now we have to warn Isobella. She has a right to know that Devon is on the loose," Wayne added.

"Maybe she can also shed some light as to why Katrina was visiting him," Kerry said.

"Exactly what I was thinking. You can ask her when you call," Wayne said.

"What?! Me?!" Kerry exclaimed.

"She seems to like you," Simon said, supporting Wayne's suggestion that Kerry should be the one to call Isobella. "And, after all, you are the one who broke the news to her when Kyle's body was found. She may feel more comfortable talking to you."

"Maybe you're right," Kerry caved. "I'll go out now."

"Call instead Kerry," Wayne suggested. "We don't have a lot of time to waste."

* * *

Isobella's phone rang seven times before she answered. Kerry thought she was either in trouble or the phone had been packed away in a box.

"Hello Doctor Dearborne," Isobella answered, clearly out of breath, "how can I help you?"

"Are you alright Isobella?" Kerry asked.

"Oh, yes. I was doing some yoga on the dock when I heard the phone ring and had to bolt up the stairs to get it," Isobella explained.

Her friendliness and calmness made what Kerry had to say even that much more difficult than she thought it would be.

"Isobella, I have some news to tell you," Kerry said.

"You sound upset," Isobella said.

"It has to do with Devon Kozlowski," Kerry said.

"The young man who killed Sebastian and his brother?" as Isobella spoke, Kerry could hear the rise in her voice.

"Yes. Him. I'm afraid he has escaped custody today," Kerry blurted out.

"How did he escape from prison?" Isobella yelled, clearly more upset than when she initially answered the call.

"He wasn't in prison, Isobella. He was in the hospital. He was in a prison fight and was being treated at the hospital for some stab wounds," Kerry explained.

"Wasn't he being watched?" Isobella asked.

"Yes, the officer was attacked during his escape," Kerry said. "But we also think he may have had some help as well."

"Yes, well, that's all well and fine. But now there is a killer on the loose!" Isobella cried.

Kerry hated to switch gears and begin asking questions about Katrina, but she knew she had to do it before Isobella hung up the phone, "Isobella, did you know that Katrina had gone to the prison to meet with Devon?"

The line fell silent, but Kerry could hear Isobella trying to control her breathing through the line.

"Isobella?" Kerry asked.

"No. I didn't know she went there," Isobella answered, barely above a whisper. "When was that?"

"A couple of days ago," Kerry said. "I was just wondering if it may shed any light on what may have prompted Devon's escape."

"I haven't spoken with Katrina for a few days. We argued about me selling Sebastian's place to Tom Pruitt. Because of the lawsuit that was going on between Sebastian and Tom. She is also finding it hard to deal with her father being murdered and knowing that Kyle has been dead all these years," Isobella explained. "She had hoped he would come back one day. She was just waiting. It must have been too much for her."

"Did she know who Devon was?" Kerry asked.

"Probably," Isobella said. "Kyle and Katrina spent a lot of time together up until the time she moved away. After you left, I was looking back at some photos, and there are many with Kyle and his friends."

"Do you remember Devon?" Kerry asked.

"Once you told me that he was in foster care I did remember one of his friends that was relatively new to the group that was living with a family in town. It must have been him," Isobella sighed. "If we had only known back then what hurt he would bring our family I would have never allowed Kyle to hang out with him."

Kerry decided to leave out the fact that she had also been to the hospital right before Devon escaped. Kerry still didn't have all the information and until she had a chance to speak with Katrina, she wasn't going to make any assumptions about why she was there.

"Isobella I want to send out an officer to be with you," Kerry said. "Unless you want to come into town."

"No. Sebastian and I spent many a night out here. I'll be fine," Isobella insisted.

"But with Devon having escaped. . ." Kerry said and then Isobella interrupted.

"He's not going to be that stupid Doctor Dearborne. I'm sure he's out of town by now," Isobella said. "Let me know when you catch him."

Kerry was about to protest but then the line went dead. Isobella had hung up and when Kerry tried to call back, she wouldn't answer the phone.

Kerry hung up the phone and turned to Wayne, "Send out an officer to watch Isobella, would you? And make sure whomever you send is prepared to be shooed away. I have a feeling that Devon hasn't left town."

CHAPTER 32

Wayne tapped his pen against the side of his computer as he read through the evidence report another time. Wayne was being pressured by several members of the community who were appalled that so much time and valuable resources were being spent in trying to find Sebastian Crow's murderer. No doubt having been spurred on by Laura Martin. Stories that had remained buried for over a decade were beginning to resurface about Sebastian Crow's violent tendencies toward his children. Rumors began to make their way around town that his aggressiveness was the reason that both his kids and wife left Lake Pines.

"I think we can all agree that Sebastian was not the most well-liked resident of Lake Pines. And I'm not going to lie, I can understand why so many people feel that he got what he deserved."

"Wayne, you know that has nothing to do with the murder investigation or the fact that Devon has escaped," Kerry said. "I'm sorry you are getting so much pressure, I'm sure that's the last thing you want or need right now. But let's use this as an opportunity to show everyone that you can be impartial in your job. You know that whole 'innocent until proven guilty' thing."

"That's what I told Laura Martin!" Wayne exclaimed.

"Let's stay focused," Simon interjected as he slid the file on Devon into the center of Wayne's desk.

"What do we know about Devon?" Kerry asked.

"Petty criminal. Mostly wiggled himself in and out of theft charges until he got wrapped up in this murder of Sebastian Crow," Wayne said.

"What about his foster family?" Kerry asked.

Wayne shrugged his shoulders, "Nothing on file that is of concern. They were a good family and gave Devon a heap of opportunity. They were just as confused as to why he ran away as anyone."

"Did you ever send anyone out to speak with them?" Kerry asked.

"No. Why would we?" Wayne asked. "They haven't seen Devon in almost fifteen years. They wouldn't be able to shed any light on Sebastian's murder. I'm not even sure they know he has been arrested."

"And you don't think it may be helpful to speak with them?" Kerry asked.

"Look, if you want to go out and speak with them, go ahead. Just take someone from the department with you so this doesn't blow back in my face," Wayne said. "Right now, I have three murders to solve, a missing prisoner and an angry widow to contend with. And that's about all I can handle."

"Don't forget the angry residents of Lake Pine," Kerry reminded him.

"Yeah, those too."

Simon agreed to tag along with Kerry when she went to speak with Devon's foster family, which appeased Wayne just enough that he didn't even want to know what she was going to ask them.

Brian and Sibyl Bernard lived on the corner of Lily Street and Fifth Avenue in a two-story Victorian-style house. The house was painted a soft yellow and had a fresh coat of bright white trim that looked as if it had been repainted that year. The lush yard was edged with gardens bursting with a mix of wildflowers and low growing shrubs, and the odd small pot randomly stuck in the ground with a mess of colorful petunias flowing over the edges. It was the kind of garden you would expect to see an old cast iron bathtub filled with dirt and flowers.

Children's toys were strewn across the yard, but not in a neglectful manner. More as if children were called in for dinner type of mess. Orange push cars, multi-colored balls, and digging toys filled the sandbox in the corner of the yard. A treehouse was built around an oak tree in the middle of the backyard and mounted to a point that was high above the roof's peak. Boards nailed in sideways and haphazard paint scheme gave the impression that it had been built by a group of children in an afternoon frenzy. But upon closer inspection, Kerry could see it was sturdily built and intentionally constructed to look like a funhouse mimicking a Dr. Suess style of architecture.

This, Kerry determined, was more than a house. It was a happy home.

Sounds of friendly group chatter and the clanging of cutlery against plates and bowls, momentarily fell silent when Kerry knocked on the door. A chair scraped against the wood floor and the dinner noises that Kerry interrupted soon began to fill the room once more. Footsteps echoed through the open screen door and Kerry and Simon were soon greeted with the smiling face of an older gentleman.

"Hello, may I help you?"

Brian Bernard was an athletic and robust-looking sixty-something-year-old man. His brown hair was salted and lightly streaked, but not yet a full shock of gray. He was the same height as Simon and a fair bit more tanned, having spent many summer hours outdoors. He pushed open the screen door and stepped out onto the porch where Kerry and Simon were standing.

"Are you Brian Bernard?" Kerry asked.

He nodded, "Yes, is everything alright?"

"My name is Kerry Dearborne. I work with the police department," Kerry learned that introducing herself as the town's coroner often frightened people and she tried to avoid it until necessary. "Officer Phillips and I would like to ask you a couple of questions about a young boy you fostered several years back."

"And who would that be?" Brian asked.

"Devon Kozlowski."

As Kerry said his name, Brian Bernard's face began to change.

"I think you both better come inside. Sibyl will want to hear whatever it is you have to say."

* * *

Sibyl was sitting in a floral armchair as Brian placed four cups of coffee, cream, and a tray of cookies on the table. After he closed the door to the living room, he joined his wife in the chair next to her.

"I'm sure this visit comes as a bit of a surprise to you both," Kerry said, "and for that I'm sorry."

"It's just a shock to hear Devon's name after all these years," Sibyl said. "I wasn't sure I would ever hear his name again."

Brian patted his wife's hand as she spoke.

"What can you tell us about Devon?" Kerry asked.

"Devon had suffered a terrible loss, and we were just so happy that we could take him into our home and give him a chance at a better life," Sibyl said. "I really hoped we could make a difference in his life."

"When was the last time you spoke with Devon?" Kerry asked.

"It was the morning he ran away," tears began to fill Sibyl's eyes and Brian handed her a tissue.

"He left for school the same time as he did every day and said that he would be hanging out with some friends after school so he may be late for dinner," Brian recalled. "When he hadn't turned up by ten o'clock, we called the police. However, because of his age and the fact that he was a foster kid. . ."

Now it was Sibyl's turn to grab her husband's hand to calm him, "Brian thinks the police were slow to react because Devon was a foster kid. That and the fact that he was only gone for a few hours, they preferred to wait."

"What eventually ended up happening with the police?" Kerry asked.

"After a couple of days of not hearing from Devon they did start to look for him, but they were never able to find him," Sibyl said.

"Did Devon give you any idea that he was thinking of running away?" Simon asked.

"No. None." Brian and Sibyl answered in unison.

Kerry and Simon glanced at each other.

"What is it?" Sibyl asked. "Have you found him?"

Her body shook and she reached for her husbands' hand to steady herself from what she was sure was bad news.

"Is he dead?" Brian forced calmness in his voice as he asked.

"Actually," Kerry said. "It's a bit more complicated than that."

CHAPTER 33

Sibyl muffled her screams in her hands. Her head shook back and forth, unwilling to believe that Devon could have killed his friend Kyle, or that he could be responsible for the murder of both Sebastian Crow as well as his brother, Calvin.

"There has to be some mistake," Brian insisted.

"I'm so sorry, but there is no mistake. We have proof that Devon was at both murder scenes, and he confessed to killing Kyle," Simon said.

"He was such a gentle boy," Sibyl said through her tears.

Kerry had heard that many times from parents of young offenders. And each time, she could momentarily see the hope in each parent's eyes that the police were wrong and that their child was not the horrible criminal that they were accused of being.

"Our problem, Mrs. Bernard, is that we urgently need to find him, and we were wondering if you had any idea where he would go if he wanted to hide. Maybe somewhere close to town," Kerry asked.

Sibyl wiped the tears from her eyes and pulled the front of her sweater down and straightened her shoulders. She took a deep breath and stood from her seat and left the room.

Kerry looked at Simon and then at Mr. Bernard, "I'm so sorry we upset your wife. We just didn't know where else to go for some answers. I know it is hard to hear, but Devon is a very dangerous man and we want to find him before anyone else gets hurt."

Just as Brian was about to answer Kerry, Sibyl walked back into the room carrying a faded white cardboard box.

She placed it on the table and lifted the lid off. Inside was a small collection of the items that Devon had amassed during the time he lived with the Bernards. School trophies and academic awards of excellence.

His baseball mitt was tucked in the side of the box. Dust covering the leather. A sign of a lost childhood and a glimpse of a once happy boy.

Kerry lifted some papers out of the box and flipped through them, hoping to get a glimpse of the murderer and what thoughts he would have had as a teen.

"What's this?" Kerry lifted out a camping badge.

"That was from the summer we convinced him to attend a fishing camp," Brian explained. "We thought it would be a good way for him to meet some new friends."

"Was he a good fisher?" Simon asked.

"A natural!" Brian beamed, and then quickly saddened remembering why Simon and Kerry were there.

Kerry spotted the corner of some photographs at the bottom of the box. She tucked her fingers under the pile and pulled them out.

There were groups of boys with their arms around each other. Each in mid-laugh, the way teen boys commonly pose for photos. There were many pictures, each in a different location, but with the same group of boys. Kerry recognized that one of the photographs was taken on the dock at Crow Island.

"I'm assuming these are the boys Devon hung out with the most," Kerry turned the photo around so that Sibyl and Brian could see what she was looking at.

"Yes," Brian said.

"Do you remember any of their names?" Simon asked.

"U-huh. The boy in the blue top is Paul. He left Lake Pines and moved to Calgary after high school. I don't know the two on the far left. That is Devon in the green top and beside him is his friend Kyle," Brian said.

"Did they have a spot they would like to go to a lot?" Simon asked. "You know, to hang out?"

"They would sometimes hang out in our treehouse, but if it was summertime they would always try and find a way to convince a parent to give them a boat and go out to the fishing cove near Beachers Bay," Brian explained. "It was where they claimed they would make the biggest catches."

"I think that is all for now," Kerry said as she began to stand. "Can I hang onto this photo?"

"Sure," Sibyl said as she replaced the other items in the box.

Simon followed Kerry's lead and thanked the Bernards as they left the room.

They showed themselves out, and they could hear Mrs. Bernard begin to cry as the front door closed behind them.

Kerry listened to the voices of the children playing in the treehouse and wondered where it all went wrong for Devon Kozlowski.

CHAPTER 34

He pulled his coat closed as the boat picked up speed, but it didn't work at keeping out the cold air. Clouds had been threatening rain all day and as Jimmy's boat sped through the channel, drops of rain began to pelt his face. He tried to shield his eyes with his left hand, but he only succeeded in creating a shelf for the rain to pool and then roll down his face.

Jimmy knew he was given a golden opportunity to redeem himself and to prove that he could be a good police officer, and this time he wasn't going to blow it. He also wasn't stupid. He knew that Constable Burgess only sent him to Crow Island to check on Isobella Frank because all the other officers were searching for Devon who had escaped under his watch.

He knew he was going to have to brace himself for the first time back at the station. The other officers would rib him about losing a prisoner, and he would have to take it. It was the way they worked. They kept each other in line and on their toes, but Jimmy knew that if he were in the line of fire that each and every one of those same guys would have his back.

But he also knew that helping secure Devon Kozlowski again would go a long way in repairing any damage he caused to his reputation.

As he neared his destination, he realized that this was his first time being at Crow Island. Ever.

In the whole time growing up in Lake Pines, he and his friends steered clear of the place. It always had the lure of the best bay for fishing and the ideal cliff for jumping, but the massive number of crows that resided on the island gave it an unsettling creepy feel that no one wanted to chance.

The boathouse was within sight and a boat was nestled inside and the door was pulled halfway down as if in preparation for a storm.

Jimmy was pulling up to the dock just as the rain began to thicken the air. Mist mixed with the rain that fell made it impossible to remain dry, even under his coat.

He quickly tied up his boat before heading up to the main cottage. A thin line of smoke crawled out from the chimney and snaked its way up, losing its trail in the clouds. The leaves, now heavy with rain, pointed to the ground and swayed with the push of the rain.

Shadows dotted the densely treed island and he could hear the echo of the caws from deep in the forest.

This place really creeped him out.

The denseness of the tree coverage provided moments of protection from the rain as Jimmy wove his way up the wooden stairs to the cottage.

The forensic team had left Crow Island and except for a few temporary posts with frayed barricade tape on the tips, there was no indication that anyone had been to the cottage for years.

Faded siding and broken windows would make any intruder think the cottage was abandoned and the unkempt lawn helpfully completed the look.

Jimmy tried to look through the window, but the grime and low light made it difficult to see through the streaked glass. The blaze that warmed the fireplace was fading and the smoke and ash smelled as if it was in its final embers, the way all late-night cottage fires eventually end up smelling like.

Jimmy walked onto the porch and shook the water from his hair before knocking on the door. The damp wood absorbed the sound of his knock and Jimmy tried again, only this time a little harder.

There was still no noise coming from inside the cottage and when he called through the screen announcing his presence, there was no response.

Jimmy slowly released his gun from the holster and opened the door.

The pressure of his first step on the wood floor gave a squeak from the bottom of his wet boot. He stepped sideways, placing his foot on the carpet next to the door.

Again, he called out Isobella's name and received no response.

Slowly, he made his way toward the fireplace and saw that it had been burned low for at least a few hours and no one had tended to the logs that slipped from their center perch.

A partially emptied glass of wine rested on an end table and when Jimmy placed the back end of his hand against the glass, he felt it was warm. It too had been sitting unattended for quite some time.

It didn't take long to check the whole cottage and realize that not only was Isobella not there but that she had left a while ago. And possibly not by choice.

Jimmy pulled his phone from his pocket and began to dial the station's number. If he was right, Isobella was gone, and she wasn't alone.

CHAPTER 35

Three murders. That was more than she could ever have imagined. Right now, she wondered what her whole life had been waiting for.

"It couldn't have been this?" she thought.

Her tears and pain had gone from a gut-wrenching ache that woke her up the last three nights, to a mind throbbing blindness that clouded every corner of her thinking.

Her panic attacks returned as well.

It had been seven years since she last had a session with Doctor Sparrow, and she tried to recall the techniques she learned all those years ago. Forcing memories into her mind that could soothe her, while trying to push the painful ones out of the way.

She knew she made the wrong decision, but what other choice did she have?

None that she could think of.

The duffle bag held most of her clothes and a few mementos from the cottage, and her purse contained her wallet, phone, and a bus ticket.

She looked at the time. She had less than an hour before the bus left and she wasn't going to miss it.

No one knew her plans and she was happy she didn't run into anyone on her way over to the island. The rain had subsided and gave her just enough time to collect what she needed and then be gone before anyone returned.

She stopped at the spot the blood-stained carpet had been cut away and removed. Residue stained the wood underneath and made it impossible to not think of what happened in this spot. It was no surprise, she thought, that it was a violent act that brought them all together again. But it was still hard to forget the moments of joy in their lives as well.

Nights of bonfires and S'More building (and eating) contests. Hours of playing Mastermind on long rainy days and of course the Crow family tradition of telling horror stories during night-time campouts.

A collection of crows, she always refused to call them a murder, currently gathered on the trees outside the porch and cawed as she stood reminiscing. It was like they knew what she had done. And was about to do.

She grabbed her bag. It was time to leave. She turned away from the roaring fire and her memories from the last few days and walked toward the front entrance.

Doors, she thought, have a strange way of presenting themselves. In her youth, the brightly painted screen door of the cottage was a welcome refuge to the end of her day. By the time she was ready to leave Lake Pines fifteen years ago, it was worn and tired and never completely closed. Today, it was that broken passage that once she passed through, she could never return.

She slung her purse across her body and slipped her arm in the handles of the duffle bag and prepared to leave.

The wine she left on the table was still cold and the fire still burning strong, and it was how she preferred to remember this place.

Before she had a chance to change her mind, she bolted from the cottage and ran the entire distance to the tin boat she left tied to the dock. She jumped from the dock and landed on the seat, tossing her bag into the front of the boat in one swift, expert move learned from a lifetime on the water.

She straddled the backbench, opened the choke, and pulled the chord. The engine sputtered to life and she yanked the end of the rope, slipping the knot loose and pushing away from the dock.

Rays of sun leaked from the clouds above, giving false hope for a clear night ahead. But experience with the weather at the lake gifted her the knowledge that she knew better.

When she was clear from the bay, she twisted her head around and glanced back at the island one final time. As she sped away from Crow Island, she could faintly hear the crows cawing and a shiver ran down her spine remembering the old family saying.

She increased the speed of the boat and headed into town. With only twenty-nine minutes to spare she knew she would have to run once she reached the Main Street dock if she was going to reach the bus station on time.

Distance was all that mattered, and she wanted as much of it as possible between her and everything that happened in Lake Pines.

Mist thickened the air over the water and her face was wet with the dampness it held. She wiped her eyes clear and squinted to make out the shape of the shoreline ahead. Soon the rain started, and as it fell it obscured the view just beyond the bow of the boat. The duffle bag began to edge up along the side of the seat and with each bounce on the water, it moved closer to falling over the side of the boat. She reached forward to grab the bag and pull it close to her feet.

In that instant, she lost control of the throttle and the boat began to sway sideways in the storm. Even if she had been paying attention, she would have been hard-pressed to avoid the boat that was positioned directly ahead of her. Shifting in the water with its lights off, the tin boat collided with its fiberglass side. She barely had time to grab hold of the side of the boat when the collision sent her flying back toward the engine.

The tin boat tipped sideways and floated in the water, taking on water with each wave. Soon it drifted toward the channel, pulled by the strong current, before coming to a sudden stop against a rocky shore. A pain shot through her leg that was jammed under the seat, and although she tried to lift it, it fell like dead weight in the boat. Rain pelted her face hard as the storm's force grew. She reached out onto the shore and pulled her body out of the battered boat and from under the broken seat, crawling over the edge and onto the sharp rocks. Using her elbows, she crawled a short distance before the pain in her leg rendered her immobile.

The rain howled and the tree branches creaked with each push of the wind as she lay on the shore. The engine of her boat was silenced in the crash and the boat's metal scrapped against the rocks, tearing at the hull with each wave.

A low hum of another boat grew closer. She turned her body around and lay on her back hoping it was the boat she collided with, and that it was coming to get her.

If she was lucky, she could get the bus first thing tomorrow morning.

She looked up at the trees as they swayed in the storm and noticed the familiar darkness that began to fill the open space on the branches.

A body leaned forward blocking the rain and slowly his face came into focus.

The last sound that could be heard before the thunder, was that of her scream and the cawing crows lined on the branches above her.

CHAPTER 36

"Finding Devon is our only priority right now," Wayne began as he briefed the room full of officers that were gathered in the small station lunchroom. "He is suspected of two recent murders and admitted to one from fifteen years ago. He is to be considered armed and very dangerous."

A few glances from fellow officers came Jimmy's way, and he did his best to ignore them. The rain had slowed the search for most of the officers and grounded the helicopter that Peter had approved for Devon's search.

"This is a manhunt, and for what it's worth, you probably won't ever see one in Lake Pines again," Wayne slipped his hands into his pockets and rocked back and forth on his boots. "No one, and I mean no one, is to go out alone. Every search, reported sighting, or sound that is investigated is to be done in pairs."

Kerry sat at the back of the room trying to be as quiet as possible surrounded by the mass of uniformed police officers. Most of the time they didn't mind her being around or even helping find evidence for some of the cases, however, this was the type of case that each of these officers trained for and hoped to get in their career. There was no way they wanted a coroner stepping on their toes. And considering how dangerous Devon turned out to be, she was fine with that.

She listened while Wayne assigned tasks and areas for the officers as they conducted their search for Devon Kozlowski. Less experienced officers were relegated to neighborhood searches in their cars and within the town's perimeter. Officers with more experience, which meant more years and not necessarily more cases, shared the assignments for the search in the forested areas as well as on the water.

Although Simon was considered a less experienced officer, he was assigned the task of a water search in and around Crow Island because of his extensive knowledge of the area. Wayne went in the boat with Simon while Sally coordinated radio feeds to the officers conducting the search.

Officer mumbled to each other as they left the room in a disorganized path. Some complaining that they were stuck driving the streets where they knew the escaped prisoner would not be seen, while other officers were fielding the search in the dense forest and out on the lake. Kerry could tell by the look on many of the officer's faces that they were just fine with their allotted assignments, especially after Officer Peterson had spent the last day avoiding the sting of having allowed the prisoner escape in the first place.

"I'm not sure if the helicopter is going to be able to assist in much of the search today," Wayne rubbed his eyes with the back of his hand. "We need to catch this guy before he gets too far away. Right now, we are looking more like a second-rate security firm than a trained police department."

"Devon is a sociopath and there is no way anyone could have prevented the three murders he is accused of being responsible for," Kerry tried to reassure Wayne with the knowledge that Devon is the way he is and it had nothing to do with the skill of the Lake Pines police. His escape, on the other hand, was a different story and she knew that was more of Wayne's concern as well.

"At least we have the helicopter available once the heavy rain lifts," Simon said as he was pulling his rain gear on over his uniform.

Wayne opened the closet at the back of the room and pulled out a raincoat and pants for himself and then pushed through a thick layer of hangers and extracted a pressed package from the back shelf. He looked at the label on the front of the bag and then tossed it to Kerry.

"This should fit you. You'll want to suit up before we get to the boat."

"You want me to come along?" Kerry asked as she caught the airborne package.

"You don't want to?" Wayne asked.

"Well, yeah."

"Then, let's go."

Wayne checked in with Sally as both Simon and Kerry waited at the front doors for him.

"So, have you decided what name we should give the dog?" Simon asked, raising one eyebrow.

"I'm not even sure we should keep it, Simon."

Simon's smile fell flat at her comment. Kerry knew how excited he was to give her the puppy and it was more than just the fact that he had wanted a pet. He thought it was one step closer to them finalizing their relationship.

Kerry let out a sigh, "I will think about it."

"Promise?" Simon asked.

"Promise what?" Wayne asked as he approached the couple.

"The puppy," Kerry said.

"Oh, that," Wayne said, preferring not to get in the middle of any relationship issues between the two people he considered friends as well as co-workers.

Wayne pulled his hat down on his head and opened the door. Simon and Kerry followed behind and the three of them faced the onslaught of the rain as it pelted them from many directions. Kerry could easily see that there was no way the helicopter would have been able to assist in the search and she had doubts about a water level search from the boat would offer any results either. But they couldn't just sit around and wait for Devon to walk into the police department.

The police boat was housed in an oversized covered boathouse a few feet from the public dock. Once they were inside the building Kerry shook the water from her jacket and removed the hood. She stepped into the back of the boat while Simon started the engine and Wayne zippered the roof closed. Kerry unzipped the raincoat and was impressed with how dry her clothes were underneath. At least she had a chance of staying warm in the rain today.

Simon pulled out of the boathouse and drove directly toward the opening in the bay that led to the east side of Lake Pines. Kerry wasn't holding out too much hope of finding Devon on the water. If he was at Crow Island, then he was long gone by now. Kerry was unsuccessful at reaching Isobella on her phone before they left. Sally offered to retry her number every few minutes by having it auto-dial through her computer system. She promised to contact Kerry if she was able to get in touch with her and would also alert her to the fact that Devon Kozlowski had not been found yet.

What really confused Kerry was the fact that Katrina had not only been to visit Devon while he was in prison but that she was also at the hospital at the same time he escaped. Kerry knew the draw for family members to the murderers of those they cared about was a common phenomenon. But Devon not only had been charged with the murder of her father, he was soon to be charged with the murder of her uncle and had also admitted to killing her brother fifteen years earlier. Wayne must have also been thinking the same thing.

"What do you think Katrina wanted from Devon?" Wayne shouted over the sound of the rain pounding on the roof of the boat.

"Morbid curiosity I assume," Kerry said. "I can understand her being drawn to the prison and wanting to confront her father and brother's killer face to face, but why go to the hospital?"

"I think she helped him escape."

"But why? He killed three people she cared about?" Kerry asked. "It doesn't make any sense."

"Nothing makes sense about this family," Wayne turned around and wiped the fog that covered the small glass window on the side of the boat.

The next fifteen minutes were spent weaving in and out of bays, through channels, and into areas around most of the main islands that Kerry didn't even know existed.

The vibrating hum of the engine slowed as Simon spotted something along the shore.

Kerry and Wayne leaned forward and looked out the front window to try and decipher the image that drew Simon's attention.

A small tin boat was tilted on its side and lodged between the shore and a pile of rocks jutting out of the water. It moved back and forth in the water, being pushed by the waves that shoved it into the shore rocks. The storm and the natural current shook the boat and it bounced up with each collision with the shoreline.

The rain created a haze over the small rocky island and Simon had to pull in close to the rocks to get a clear view. As he neared the rocks, he tilted the engine and Wayne pulled the roof back and hung over the side of the boat.

He grabbed hold of the swaying boat and stepped out onto the rocky shore. Rain had slicked the surface of the shore and forced Wayne to walk around the back of the boat where the surface was a little flatter. Wayne jumped from the rocks and onto the grassy edge of the shore where his footing was more secure. From there he could see the splintered wood from the seats on the boat and the battered engine that hung on one bolted clamp on the rear of the boat.

Kerry pulled the hood of her jacket over her head and walked along the same path that Wayne did and came to a stop beside him.

The front of the boat was badly dented and the force of whatever this small tin runabout hit sent a rippling shock through the hull. The trim that lined the top edge of the boat was bent and hanging off the right side of the boat and wavered in the pull of the water. Gashes were clear along the sides where the sharp rocks tore at the metal, thin with age. Water filled the boat, now tipped on one side holding it between the gully of rocks.

A duffle bag rested near the cracked seat at the back of the boat, heavy with the water it absorbed. Kerry stepped forward and balanced herself on the edge of the rocks next to the battered boat. She reached forward and tugged at the handles on the bag until it was close enough to lift out.

She unzipped the bag and removed the small purse that was tucked in the side. Inside was the owner's wallet, along with a ticket for a bus that left ten minutes earlier.

There was no need to check the identification cards in the wallet because under the purse was a photo of

Katrina and Kyle laughing as they sat around a bonfire roasting marshmallows and sitting at Sebastian's feet as he smiled down at them.

The downpour couldn't mask the gray ashen color of Wayne's face and his concern that another Crow family murder victim would soon be found. And even though most of the blood had been washed away by the rain, it was clear from the red-lined cracks on the splintered oar that it was not the accident that stained the wood. But whoever had arrived and took Katrina away.

CHAPTER 37

Three murders and one suspicious missing person, all from the same family had established that this was more than a coincidence. Even an amateur sleuth could have figured this one out, but what didn't make sense was why Devon Kozlowski had such an obsession with the Crow family in the first place, and why his anger took such a murderous turn.

Wayne called Sally and described the boat accident, who then, in turn, dispatched a forensic team to the site.

"Outside of the boat and the oar, I don't think we are going to get much from this area," Kerry said.

"I don't think it's going to come as any surprise that I'm guessing that it's Devon who is responsible for attacking Katrina," Wayne rubbed his hands together and then blew into his palms to warm them. "And we have no real way of figuring out where this kid is. He had no real ties to Lake Pines, and he hasn't been in contact with his foster family either."

"And Sally hasn't had any luck trying to reach Isobella, and now it's clear that it's a matter of life and death," Kerry added.

She was worried that they weren't going to be able to reach Isobella in time to warn her, and it was a real possibility that it was too late already.

The police stationed at Crow Island said that she had not returned and that there was no indication that Isobella packed up and left. From the condition of the cottage, it appeared as if Isobella was going to walk through the doors at any moment.

Wayne instructed the two officers to remain at the cottage until further notice. And from the sounds of the reports coming in from the other officers who were conducting searches, the two officers at Crow Island had the warmest and driest detail of all.

"Do you remember when old man Jarvis was killed when we were teenagers?" Simon asked Wayne as he drove the boat toward town.

"Yeah, there was a manhunt that whole summer. None of our parents wanted any of us out in groups of less than four and no one was allowed out past dark," Wayne recalled.

"What happened?" Kerry asked.

"This guy who ran a fishing camp about an hour north of here was killed when he was opening up his cottage. I don't even know what his real name was, everyone just called him *old man Jarvis*. Anyway, he was found by a few of the summer staff who had arrived to help him get the cabins on the island ready for guests who were booked in for the start of the summer season. He had been dead for a few days by the time his body was found, and the police searched most of the summer for his killer. Everyone was terrified that year," Simon explained.

"Was his killer ever found?" Kerry asked, her interest piqued.

Wayne shook his head and laughed, "He was a drifter who had found his way out to the island hoping for some food, lodging, or a job or something. Turns out he had been holed up in one of the cabins on the far end of the island the whole time the police were searching for him. He was a little more than a hundred feet from the murder, and he managed to stay hidden in the dense landscape."

"That's it!" Kerry shouted.

"What's it?"

"The picture that we got from Devon's foster family. The one at the fishing camp the boys used to go to. It's the only place that Devon seemed to have any connection to during his short time in Lake Pines."

"Where was it again?" Simon asked out loud. He could recall the photograph but not if the Bernards told them where it was. In fact, he knew they didn't because they had no reason to ask.

"I'll have Sally pull the file from your desk," Wayne started to dial his phone.

"Forget it. We are only a few minutes away now. It'll be faster if we look ourselves. We need to get back and see if we can figure out where that picture was taken."

The deluge of rain ended, and the helicopter was just leaving the helipad as Simon pulled the boat into the slip. The only saving grace with the rain having ended is that there may not be much lake traffic and the pilot would have an easier time searching the area for any movement.

Simon and Kerry tossed their wet coats on the chair next to Simon's desk and Wayne pulled his off and draped it over the back of his seat.

It was close to three in the afternoon and the break in the clouds allowed a blast of the afternoon sun to warm the room. There would still be enough light for a few more hours and Kerry hoped it would be enough to conduct a thorough search of the area.

Simon pulled three photos from the file and lay them face up on his desk.

"These are the ones we got from the Bernards," Simon explained. "There's nothing written on the back indicating where or when these photos were taken."

A young Devon smiled into the photos. Friends and buddies with their arms draped around each other, not realizing that fifteen years later they would be used in a search to find a killer. Each photo was taken in the same location indicating that it was an area that the friends enjoyed returning to and one that was safe to assume held some meaning for all of them.

Right now, they hoped it held some meaning for Devon and that he would decide to take refuge there while he was being hunted by the police.

"Do you recognize this spot?" Kerry asked both Simon and Wayne as they stared at the faded images.

They both shook their heads.

"The pictures are just focused on the kids and not any surrounding buildings or distinct features of the landscape. This could be anywhere!" Wayne, frustrated with the search, slammed his hands on the metal desk.

Sally was walking behind him with a tray holding three hot coffees when he startled her. She jumped slightly and the tray of coffees tumbled to the floor splashing against Wayne's leg and the edge of the desk.

"Oh, geez!" Sally yelped.

She grabbed the small napkins from the tray and began to help dab the coffee spill from the top of Simon's desk, "I'm so sorry guys," she said as she quickly wiped the spill.

"Don't worry Sally," Wayne said. "It was my fault too."

Sally dabbed the spill as it began to run across the surface of the desk and started to get close to the pictures. She glanced at the images and then grabbed one of the photographs from the desk and asked, "Is this Devon when he was younger?"

"Yeah, we are trying to figure out where these photos were taken, on the off chance he's hiding-out there," Simon explained. "Do you recognize any of them?"

Sally grabbed a second photo and looked at the two side by side, "Not the people. The place. It's Trappers Camp off Elk Bay. See the logo on their bags."

They leaned forward and looked closely to where Sally referenced, and they too could see the head of the walleye encircled with rope. The image was faded but still visible.

"It was so small we almost missed it," Wayne said.

"We did miss it," Kerry added. "Where is this camp?"

"It's been closed for over a decade now, I'm not even sure who owns it," Wayne said. "It's about a thirty-minute boat ride from here, and if we leave now, we may have a chance to get there before dark."

"And hopefully we will find Devon there as well," Simon said.

They ran from the station and headed down to the boat that they had just docked. As Kerry jumped from the dock into the boat, she prayed for three things.

That the rain would hold off.

That Devon was at Trappers Camp.

And that Isobella and Katrina weren't with him.

CHAPTER 38

Trappers Camp sat on an unnamed island in Elk Bay. The island was densely covered with birch trees and large jack pines lined the shore and stretched over the water. A few broken boards were all that remained of the cribs that once held up a substantial dock. Logs, weathered over the years, jutted out of the surface of the water at various angles. Piles of rocks were still nestled in the base of each crib and most broke the surface of the water.

Crayfish came to the surface of the rocks and with the break in the rain, they sat perched in the warmth of the late day sun. A blue heron balanced on one of its spindly legs atop of one of the broken cribs and took flight when Simon drove up next to it. Waves crashed against the cribs and sprayed up a white foam that lay trapped on the rocks along the surface of the shore.

Dampness from the rain still held a chill in the air and Kerry shivered as the boat came to a stop. Simon jumped out the front of the boat and secured it to a tree on the shore. The lack of a dock made it impossible to park anywhere else.

There was no sign of any other boat having been pulled up along the shore on the side of the island that faced Elk Bay. The island was just over ten acres and had no other inhabitants registered to it. Trees that had felled over the years due to storms and beavers taking their pick for their dams, lay rotting on the ground.

The damp smell of pine mixed with decomposing leaves was not enough to mask the wafting scent of rotting fish from the carcasses the pelicans had pulled up on the pebble shore to feast on through the summer. Hollowed out shells of crayfish and bones of small fish lined the stony beachfront. The island was a veritable haven for lake wildlife and Kerry was glad to see some parts of the lake could be left untouched, no matter how bad the smell was.

A small climb from the shore brought them to a landing close to the original lodge. The center of the roof was bowed in, and holes were noticeable from where they stood. Large wooden beams were visible through the breaks in the roof and although the abandoned building was clearly dilapidated, the structure was remarkably straight.

Fallen pine needles had killed the grass that most likely had once covered the flat ground around the lodge, and small tree shoots had pierced the field leading from the forest to the shoreline. Rock beds that held welcoming gardens were caved in at their base and both weeds and eroded dirt filled the space.

Chairs still lined the oversized porch and due to their size and weight had remained unmoved and un-toppled for the many years they were neglected. Dirt and mold coated the wood and a green tinge supplanted the amber color of the pine from which they were constructed.

Cracked glass, barely held in place with window putty that had split and shrunk over the years, were coated with a thick layer of grime and dust making it impossible to see inside the lodge. Kerry was surprised to find the front door locked when she turned the tarnished brass handle.

They made their way around to the rear of the building and found the door ajar. The wood around the door frame and handle was splintered and cracked from having been forced open, although not recently. Tracks from animals and intruders of the teenage ilk left a trail of mud, scat, and empty beer cans strewn across the floor.

Simon shone his flashlight ahead of the group as they searched the entire main lodge. Although not intended to be used as a hotel, the lodge had ten bedrooms all situated on the top floor. Two main bath areas were situated at each end of the upper level and had also revealed traces of intruders, who had left (among other things) garbage and broken glass on the floor.

"It doesn't look like anyone has been here for several years," Simon scanned his flashlight around the main living room on the ground floor. Dust covered the remaining furniture and floors and the walls were adorned with photographs of guests and their proud catches during their trip.

"This place looks like it was quite popular when it was open," Kerry walked the length of the room looking at each photograph hoping to glean an image of Devon and his friends but failed to find any trace of him in any of the pictures.

"Look at this," Wayne was standing next to the front door. Hanging from a small nail in the knotty pine paneling was a map held in a crooked frame. It was a map of the island that directed guests to the individual cabins on the property. A small dock stretched out from a sandy crescent beach on the backside of the island and was most likely where Devon would have parked if he was here. And at the bottom right-hand corner of the map was the logo that Sally recognized in the photograph.

The cabins were situated in a semi-circle pattern with the main lodge located in the center.

"The trees must be hiding them from view. I didn't see any of them when we came up from the water," Kerry tucked her hands in her pockets to try and warm them up.

"Let's get going and check them out before it gets too dark."

Simon unlocked the front door and they left the main lodge. There were eight cabins in total each about thirty feet apart, offering privacy to their guests. The first five showed no signs of trespassing and had avoided the attention of both animals and teenagers over the years. The sixth cabin was the victim of some storm destruction since the island had been abandoned, however, it also had the best view of the lake because of where it was positioned.

As they neared the seventh cabin Simon suddenly stopped and crouched down. Kerry and Wayne followed suit. Simon turned his head and whispered behind him, "I heard a sound over there. I'm sure I heard voices."

Wayne nodded to Simon and stepped in front of Kerry. They continued to approach the cabin, this time, taking each step very quietly. The ground was covered with branches and leaves and each step threatened to reveal their position. The rain which softened much of the noise from the ground was protected from reaching the area where they were currently walking making each crunch beneath their feet seem even louder.

The sun was beginning to set as they neared the back of the cabin. As they walked out from the cover of the trees Kerry could hear two voices. One was that of a man's and the cries unquestionably that of a woman.

A light shone from the inside of the cabin stretching the shadow of the man inside across the window making him seem larger than he was. He paced the length of the cabin and passed in front of the window several times, however, because of the angle from where they were standing it was difficult to determine if for certain it was Devon.

"Remember, we still don't know who was with Devon the night he killed Sebastian," Wayne warned.

With all their focus on catching Devon, Kerry almost forgot that they thought that Devon was working with someone else and very little of their energy went into finding out who that person might have been.

Wayne and Simon both drew their guns and held them in front of their bodies as they approached the cabin door. At least, Kerry figured, with one door there was no way of Devon, or whomever else was inside, easily escaping.

They crouched under the window frame as they crept toward the door. The porch was small and was one step up from the ground. Even after all the years from when it was originally built there were no squeaks or creaks when they stepped on the boards, hopefully affording them the element of surprise.

Wayne and Simon positioned themselves on each side of the door jamb and Kerry stepped behind Simon, staying far from the edge of the entrance.

Simon nodded and then Wayne turned the handle and together they rushed through the door. The noise of the door exploding open caught those inside completely by surprise. Screams and yells followed shouts from Wayne and Simon and within a minute there was silence.

CHAPTER 39

Kerry peered around the edge of the door. Wayne and Simon were standing on each end of the cabin facing Devon who had his arm wrapped around Katrina's neck and a gun in the other. He moved the gun rapidly as he spoke, aiming at both Katrina and Isobella with each move.

"I'll shoot if you take one step closer!" he yelled.

Wayne held his gun positioned on Devon, "There is nowhere to go Devon. Don't make it worse than it needs to be."

"What would you know!" he shouted.

"I know that things haven't been great for you since you initially ran away from Lake Pines," Wayne took one step closer.

Devon stepped back and screamed at both he and Simon, "I told you to not move!"

Wayne stood still, "You need to let these women go. They have done nothing wrong to you."

Simon took one step to the right as Devon was focusing his eyes on Wayne.

"That's the problem," Devon answered through his tears. "They did nothing."

Simon slid his foot sideways, this time Devon caught his movement.

Devon moved the gun and fired at the floor at Simon's feet and then pushed the gun against the side of Isobella's head. Isobella struggled against the ropes that bound her to the chair and her muffled cries for help were stifled by the tape that covered her mouth.

"I can't go back to prison!" Devon cried.

"We can get you some help," Wayne promised. "Whatever it is that you have been through there are people who can help you."

A laugh burst through Devon's frantic cries, "Like when I needed it when I was younger. Yeah, right."

"No one else needs to die tonight Devon," Wayne pleaded. "And that includes you."

"Please let me go," Katrina's words struggled through her sobs as she wrestled to free herself from Devon's grasp.

"Hasn't she lost enough?" Wayne asked.

Devon's face changed. The tense anger was replaced with exhaustion.

"In the course of a few days, she has learned her father, uncle, and younger brother were all killed. She doesn't deserve this," Wayne sensed he was getting through to him.

Devon relaxed his arm and lowered the gun away from the side of Isobella's head, but still held it firmly in his grasp.

"Think about it, Devon. She had been waiting fifteen years hoping for her brother to return, and now she has nothing left to hope for. Her father, brother, and uncle are all gone. Let her go," Wayne watched as Devon's arm loosened the hold around Katrina's neck.

She pushed herself away from his body and fell to the floor in a heap of sobs.

CHAPTER 40

Scraping sounds from Simon and Wayne's boots were followed by the familiar noise of someone being wrestled to the ground. Low, soft sobs came from inside the cabin.

Kerry stepped out from where she was hiding and walked inside. Isobella was tied to an old wooden chair and Devon had fallen to the ground to his knees and had buried his face in his hands, the gun having been kicked aside by Wayne.

Sitting on the floor was Katrina. Her back was pressed up against the wall of the cabin and her knees were pulled up tight against her chin. Her face was buried deep in her arms that were wrapped tightly around her legs. Her whole body convulsed with each muffled sob. Kerry rushed over to Katrina and wrapped her arms around her shoulders.

"It's okay, we got you," Kerry whispered as she tried to calm Katrina down.

Her clothes were still soaked wet with the rain and the recent accident in her tin boat. Kerry grabbed a blanket that was hung over the back of an oversized rustic chair that was positioned next to the empty fireplace hearth and wrapped it around Katrina's body. Kerry rubbed her hands over Katrina's back and arms trying her best to calm her body from its shivers. Although she was sure it was more than the damp cold that caused her body to shake.

Small traces of blood matted the hair behind her left ear where a two-inch gash protruded through the skin and Kerry recalled the splintered oar that lay on the rocks near her battered boat.

Kerry looked back at Devon and through his sobs, she was certain she heard him scream '*I can't. I can't*', and as she glanced up, it was the look on Isobella's face that frightened her more.

CHAPTER 41

Isobella was wrapped in an old dusty blanket that was pulled from the bed and rubbed her wrists where the ropes had tugged at her arms. She shivered as Wayne took her report and full account of what had happened over the last few hours, trying to not interrupt her as she spoke.

"Just try and take a step back," Wayne tried his best to calm Isobella down so he could get a clear account of what happened over the last few hours.

"He killed him. He killed Sebastian!" Isobella shouted.

"I know Isobella," Wayne told her. "We've been trying to track him down ever since he escaped custody. We went to your cottage to try and warn you, but you were already gone."

Isobella stared up at Wayne and her eyes were glossed over in fright, "He. Killed. Him." She continued to mumble pausing between each word in a staccato motion.

"She's in shock, Wayne," Kerry said. "Let's wait until we get her back into town."

Simon had taken Devon down to the dock, securely handcuffed to await the police who were on their way to collect him. Once he was safely handed off to the officers Simon was going to return and help get Isobella back into the boat and into town.

All of them agreed that having Isobella, Katrina, and Devon travel back to town in the same boat was not a great idea. An extra team was called to the island to collect the boat that Devon brought Isobella and Katrina in. They were instructed to tow it back into town so it could be properly examined.

"I don't want any loose ends on this one," Wayne warned the officers. "This may seem like an open and shut case, but remember, we have three murders and two kidnappings that this guy is up against."

The officers left and once Simon returned to the cabin, Kerry and Wayne would be ready to leave with Isobella and Katrina.

Kerry knelt next to Isobella and rubbed her back. Isobella jumped at the touch and snapped her head toward Kerry. When she realized it was Kerry beside her, Isobella let out a sigh of relief, and the tension released from her shoulders.

Her tears streaked the blue liner under her eyes, and it ran down the front of her cheeks. The rims of her eyes were flamed red. Her bottom lip quivered as she blinked away tears and she whispered to Kerry, "It was him."

Kerry grabbed both of Isobella's hands, now was not the time to grill her with too many questions.

"We have him now Isobella. He can't hurt anyone else," Kerry assured her. "We just need to know what happened today. When Officer Peterson arrived at your cottage to let you know he had escaped, you weren't there. He found an empty cottage and a half-burned fire. Can you tell us what happened and how you got out here?"

"I was on my way back from town. Katrina and I were going to have a quiet dinner. Our last dinner in the cottage before it sold," Isobella took a deep breath and wiped her eyes, seeming to have composed herself slightly. "I was walking back to my boat when I saw him. He was standing right there in the middle of the pier like no one could touch him. Like he hadn't done anything wrong."

"What did you do then?" Kerry asked.

"I freaked out is what I did! I couldn't believe it," Isobella closed her eyes and shook her head. "He said he killed them. He killed Sebastian." Isobella began to sob at the mention of Sebastian's name.

"Maybe we should wait until we are back in town," Wayne interjected.

"No!" Isobella snapped. "You need to promise me he won't get out. He's a monster!"

"Officer Phillips is handing him off to two officers who are taking him directly to the jail. He won't be getting any leniency this time, you can be sure of that," Wayne promised.

Just at that moment, Simon had walked into the cabin, "Whenever you are ready, we can go. Peterson just picked up Devon and soon he will be securely locked away."

Isobella sat up straight and stared straight ahead. The dusty blanket fell away from her left shoulder, and she straightened her back and momentarily seemed to have pulled herself together. She stood from the wooden chair and kicked aside the ropes that had bound her arms together.

She looked directly into Wayne's eyes, "Let's get out of this place and you can take whatever report you need. Just as long as you promise he will never get out."

Wayne nodded and stepped aside and Isobella walked directly toward the door, never once looking back.

CHAPTER 42

Jimmy drove at full speed as he headed back to town with Devon Kozlowski safely handcuffed in the seat behind him. Officer Jones was sitting next to him, making sure he had no plans of escaping or attacking Jimmy again, and the stolen gun from his patrol car was safely secured in a sealed evidence bag. That was the worst part. Being hit over the head and knocked out cold while a prisoner escaped was no match for the feeling Jimmy experienced when he realized his spare gun and rifle were in his patrol car, and eventually in Devon's possession. A cop's stolen gun is any officer's worst nightmare, especially if it ends up being used in a crime.

A shiver ran up Jimmy's spine as he thought of the consequences he was going to face for having his keys as well as his weapon stolen. He was sure to suffer a suspension, but that was a far cry better than someone having been killed with it.

It took all the professionalism that Jimmy tried to instill upon himself as a police officer not to slug Devon for knocking him out and escaping custody at the hospital. He just kept telling himself that it would feel so much better to waltz into the station with Devon in handcuffs and book him into custody. This time for the final time.

Actually, Jimmy was prepared to be peppered with an assault of taunts from Devon. That's how most punks would react when having been recaptured by an officer they escaped from earlier. It's as if they always understood the ridicule that police suffered from other officers, with a misstep in their duty. But instead, Devon sat quietly looking out over the water as the boat traveled toward town.

Tears rolled down Devon's face and in an instant, he transformed from a murderous convict into a vulnerable child. Jimmy almost felt sorry for him, or sympathetic, or whatever it was he was feeling. It just wasn't hatred.

They arrived at the dock and walked the short distance to the station in silence. They entered the station to an equally quiet atmosphere, and everyone watched as Jimmy began to hand Devon over to an officer who was going to officially record his arrest.

Jimmy listened as the officer had made sure Devon understood the charges against him and asked him if his rights were read to him during his arrest on the island.

To each of those questions, he answered a soft and muted 'yes'.

Each question and each step of his arrest was recorded and passed without incident. Opposite of what Jimmy had prepared himself for.

As he was being led to a cell, he stopped just before he stepped inside. He slowly turned and faced the officer who was walking him back and looked over his shoulders and directly at Jimmy who was watching.

"There's just one thing you got wrong, officer."

"What's that?" Jimmy asked.

"My name is not Devon Kozlowski. It's Kyle. Kyle Crow."

CHAPTER 43

It was getting dark outside and the storm had completely passed over Lake Pines. Isobella was sitting in an interview room holding a hot cup of coffee in a paper cup and still wrapped in the dusty blanket from the cabin where she was being held.

Isobella's head hung low and her chin rested against her chest. Tears ran from her face and the anxious shock that registered when she was first rescued was replaced with a sense of dread and loss. She had been hollowed out in the absolute worst way a person can be. By the loss of those around them. Isobella was now left totally and completely alone with a feeling of dread, betrayal, and isolation.

When Isobella walked onto the pier in preparation for her dinner with her daughter and glanced into Kyle's eyes, the events of the last few weeks all fell together. She knew in an instant that it was Kyle who had killed Sebastian as well as his uncle Calvin. Without any words spoken between them, she knew it was not Kyle found in that mudslide but his young friend Devon Kozlowski.

The pit of her stomach ached as she looked into Kyle's eyes after fifteen years and saw pure, raw hatred.

She said nothing. There was nothing she could say. Nothing she could think of saying.

They stared at each other for what seemed an eternity. A mother and a son each on a side of a battle that neither could have seen coming many years ago. Yet, here they were.

Kyle's fingers wrapped around the handle of a small gun and he slowly raised it toward her. With no words he waved the gun toward the boat, motioning her to walk ahead of him.

Isobella strode toward her boat and held her head high, looking forward. She walked past Kyle and placed her grocery bags in the boat. Kyle untied the front ropes while Isobella loosened the back one.

Isobella started the engine and pulled out of the slip. She drove slowly as she headed toward Crow Island. Where else would he expect to go tonight? It all made sense. However, she was unsure of what she was going to say or do when they arrived.

The rain began to pour and obstructed her view over the water and made driving the boat even more difficult, despite her knowledge of the water. Having a gun pointed at your back by your child will do that. Tears that hadn't flowed for many years came now like a torrent in her eyes. Memories of a more peaceful moment in their lives were destroyed over the last few days, and minutes, with the realization that Sebastian was gone. And that Kyle had killed him. She blinked her eyes hoping to clear her vision, but the rain continued to swirl around her face, pelting her harder as she drove.

Unable to see the waves, her boat collided sideways with the whitecaps pushing the boat into the air and slamming it down onto the surface of the water. She and Kyle were tossed around in the boat, their arms bouncing on the sides of the windows.

A howling gust blew directly at her face and Isobella instinctively covered her head with her right arm, causing her to lose control of the steering of the boat and relinquishing control of the vessel to the violent current. Just as she tried to regain control of the steering, the force of the crash pulled Isobella to the floor of the boat. A combination of the blinding storm and the hit to her head disoriented her. She rolled onto her stomach and lay on the bottom of the boat trying to catch her breath.

She began to feel the boat move and thought that the waves were carrying them away in the current.

She looked toward the front of the boat and saw Kyle behind the wheel. He was steering the boat slowly and maneuvering around the waves. He came to an expected stop. When Isobella looked up she saw a line of trees hanging over the boat. He had pulled along the shoreline and was climbing out of the boat.

Isobella waited until he was out of the boat and then she forced herself up and stumbled toward the gears. She was just about to put the boat in reverse when she noticed Kyle on the shore and standing over a body that was sprawled on the ground. A tin boat bounced against the rocks and the shore being pushed by the waves. She didn't immediately recognize the boat, but she recognized the bag that was floating in the water. It was Katrina's.

Dazed and confused, Isobella stumbled over the edge of the boat and across the slippery rocks and then rushed toward Katrina's screams.

Just as she reached them Kyle swung the oar. Isobella fell to her knees and crawled toward her daughter. She threw her body on top of Katrina's and yelled at her to wake up, but her head fell to the side and she didn't move.

Kyle pulled Isobella away from Katrina's body and dragged her to the boat. He then returned to where

Katrina lay and dragged her body along the same rough rocks and pulled her into the boat.

From that point on Isobella said everything was a haze. Kyle brought her to the old fishing camp he used to go to with his friends and there, he said, he was going to kill them both.

Wayne, Simon, and Kerry sat in silence as Isobella recounted the events of the day and the horrifying experience of watching her daughter lay motionless in the bottom of the boat, unsure if she was still alive.

When Isobella was finished speaking she sank back in the gray metal chair and wrapped the blanket around her shoulders.

Silence filled the space between them for a few minutes in the hollow interrogation room before Kerry asked, "Do you have any idea why Kyle was filled with so much hatred for your whole family?"

Instead of giving her an answer Isobella buried her face in her hands and broke down into a violent sob.

CHAPTER 44

Katrina held the pack of ice against the back of her head. The painkillers had not dulled the ache and Kerry's cleansing of the wound only added to the sharp stinging sensation she was feeling now. The ice wavered over the large bump that was forming behind her ear and she moved it around for a few minutes until she found the angle where it rested more easily.

The change of clothes that Kerry found in the police station did little to warm Katrina's body and calm her shivers. Her hair was still wet, but the truth was, it was the brutal realization that Kyle was a murderer that made her uneasy.

She tried to deal with the horror of her father having been murdered by facing his killer. It would turn out to be the worst decision she would ever make in her life.

Her therapist had encouraged her, through her years of sessions, that trying to confront her fears was the only way to overcome them.

She wondered what Doctor Sparrow's advice would be tonight.

She was unprepared for the shock or the turn her life would take the moment she came face to face with her father's alleged killer.

When the prisoner was seated across from her, on the other side of the plexiglass window, all of Katrina's resolve fell to the wayside. She was thrown back into her youth when she would try and protect her younger brother from the punches and hits that would befall him for the slightest misstep he would make.

Careful to not let any bruising or marks land on an area that would be easily visible, layers of tender skin and small cigarette burns lay silently under themed t-shirts and colorful tops. Marks that told the true tale of the Crow family. Marks, that if seen, would have torn them apart.

Kyle convinced her that their father's murder was an accident and that he never meant for any of it to happen. He frightened Katrina with stories of violence and threats against his life in prison. He begged her for her help, he needed to get out.

Reluctantly, she agreed but was unsure of how she was going to help him. She was a nurse earning a decent salary, but she made nothing close to what would be needed to hire a decent lawyer to defend him out of the mess he was in.

Kyle told her that he wouldn't need a lawyer and she could help him from a safer position.

She didn't know how he was going to manage it, but Kyle said he was going to get moved to another location where she would be able to help him escape.

When she pressed for more information, Kyle just said, *"Be at the hospital tomorrow and you'll see."*

Wayne rested his arms on the table and lay his pen on the pad of paper. He crossed his arms, "You have been through a lot Katrina. Why don't we get Doctor Dearborne to take you to the hospital to get checked out, and maybe get that cut stitched up? We can finish up with any more questions tomorrow if need be."

Wayne pushed his chair back and stood up.

Katrina lowered her arm that held the bag of ice to the table, "Am I going to be arrested for helping Kyle escape?"

Wayne folded his arms in front of his body, "Normally, yes. But I think there are extenuating circumstances at play here. We can probably let you off with a warning and maybe some community service."

A relieved look came across Katrina's face and she thanked Wayne before she followed him out of the room.

She walked down the hall toward the exit and paused outside the room where Isobella was waiting.

She glanced inside and then without saying a word she turned and headed out the door to where Kerry was waiting to take her to the hospital.

CHAPTER 45

Kyle Aloysius Crow had sat in his cell for an hour before he was brought into an interrogation room. The case held an endless stream of questions, and at the same time, it was very clear. Kyle Crow was responsible for a total of three deaths, two kidnappings, and attempted murder, along with the charges of escaping custody. None of which seemed to concern him. Although a lawyer was offered to him, it was refused. As the charges were being read, he didn't refute them.

There was no accomplice in the death of Sebastian Crow, and as it was now clear, it was not a robbery gone wrong, as Wayne had initially assumed.

Kyle had learned the art of self-defense from the first member of his family he killed. His father. A quick short jab to his neck had severed his artery and killed him instantly. The seven stab wounds, well, that was the drive of pure painful emotion. The anger and hatred had spilled out when he saw his father laying on the floor.

The man who was supposed to protect him but failed miserably.

Kyle hadn't planned on killing his father, in fact, he hadn't planned on killing anyone. I guess that's how most murders go.

"Why don't you start at the beginning," Wayne instructed his prisoner.

"That's what I'm doing," Kyle explained.

"No, I mean fifteen years ago when you killed Devon Kozlowski."

"Oh, that," he mumbled.

"Yeah, that."

"Devon and I went to school together. He was a quiet kid, but he had a lot of problems. His foster family was nice, but he overheard them talking and he was sure he was being moved off to another home in Sudbury. He didn't want to be shuffled off again so we both decided to leave town. To run away."

"Where were you planning to go?"

"We were going to stay with Katrina in Toronto."

Kyle dropped his face and an awkward silence filled the room.

"Why did you want to run away?" Wayne asked.

Kyle stared at his shoes and began to fiddle with his hands.

"Was it because of the abuse Kyle?" Simon asked.

He raised his face to his and nodded.

Wayne asked, "Then what happened?"

"We met at the hill where we normally hung out and we were going to hide there until it was time to catch the bus, but Devon began to backtrack and said he changed his mind."

"Why?"

"He said he confronted his foster parents and they said they were actually speaking with a lawyer about filing the paperwork to officially adopt him, not to move him along. They were going to Sudbury to file the paperwork because they were told it would be faster to do it through that district office. He was all tears and crying saying he finally found a family again."

"So, why kill him?" Wayne asked.

Kyle lifted his head, "I didn't mean to. He began to walk down the hill and I went to grab him. We started to wrestle, and he landed a punch on my face and began to walk away. I grabbed his neck from behind and pulled him toward me and I heard a snap. That's when he fell back and hit his head against a rock. Once I realized he was dead I knew I couldn't call the police, so I buried him and took his identification and took the first bus out of town."

"How did you bury him if all you had was a backpack?"

"There was road construction that year and the crew kept a shed with their tools by the side of the road. I grabbed a shovel and buried him along with my backpack before I left."

Wayne let out a deep sigh. "Then why come back?"

Kyle shrugged his shoulders, "I wanted to see my dad. To see if I could somehow repair the split. I realized they sold the family home but after a few days I tracked him down at the cottage."

"How did you know he'd be there if the house was sold?"

"My uncle told me," Kyle said.

"The same uncle you shot?" Wayne asked.

"Let's get back to your dad," Simon said. "When did he realize you were back?"

"I followed him to the grocery store and when he came out, I called his name from where I was waiting in the park just before the docks. He was shocked to see me. He was happy but shocked. He started to go off and talk about calling my mom and getting everyone together, but it was too much. I freaked out. He told me it was fine, and we just sat and talked about where I had been over the last fifteen years."

"So, how'd the conversation go from a joyful homecoming to where you ended up killing your dad?"

"I had let it slip that my uncle had been sending me money while I was gone. You know, to help me out. He got really angry for us both letting him think I was in danger or dead."

"I can understand that," Wayne said.

"Do you know he refused to move away from Lake Pines in case I returned?" Kyle said. He wiped the tears that began to form in his eyes.

"So again, how'd it go so wrong?"

"Well, that's when we started yelling and during our fight, I let it slip that Devon and I were going to run away but that Devon actually died that night by accident. That's when he took off. He ran down to his boat and went to the cottage. My uncle was waiting around the corner because he knew that I was going to let my dad know I was back in Lake Pines. They got into a fight, a short one, but I heard him yell at Uncle Calvin to stay out of his business."

"That must be when they were overheard arguing on the street," Simon said to Wayne.

"What happened next?" Wayne asked.

"I followed him out to the island later that night. I knew he'd have the place locked up, so I used the trap door he built in the floor and came inside that way. I tried to talk to him, but he said he needed to call my mom, and then they needed to call the police about Devon."

"And I'm assuming that's when you freaked out and killed your dad?" Wayne said.

"How could he wait all those years and then turn around and turn me in?" Kyle sobbed.

"Because what you did was wrong Kyle," Simon said. "No matter how mad you were with your dad when you left, you have to understand that?"

Kyle squinted his eyes as he glanced at Simon, "I never said I left because I was mad at my dad."

Wayne decided to steer the conversation back to the current timeline, "So after you killed Sebastian what did you do?"

"I was freaking out, so I went straight to my uncle's place. I was a mess, crying and yelling. Once I calmed down, I told him what happened, and he just fell apart. My dad was his best friend. He fell back in his chair and just cried like a baby. Then he just snapped out of it and became super angry. He threatened to call the police, and he said he was going to make sure I paid for killing his brother."

"And, that's when you shot your uncle," Wayne said.

Kyle nodded.

The remainder of the interrogation continued similarly as Kyle explained Katrina's visit to the jail. She initially wanted to confront Devon and ask why he would have killed her dad and brother, but the second she looked at his face she recognized him.

Kyle had convinced Katrina not to tell their mother and to also help him escape. He was her brother and she knew what he had been through and was sympathetic to the trauma he suffered. That and the fact that she just wanted her brother to be safe.

Eventually, Kyle explained his plan on getting admitted into the hospital where she could sneak in and help him escape. She grabbed a set of her father's old skeleton keys that unlocked most locks and snuck into his hospital room as a nurse.

It didn't take long for Katrina to regret her decision and she told Kyle he was on his own and that she was leaving town and didn't want to hear from him again.

Their boats colliding was by complete chance and as she lay on the rocks screaming, Kyle knew that she would never let him be free.

"I read the reports, Kyle, of when the police and social services were called to your home to investigate accusations of you being hit by your father," Wayne said. "So even though it is still a crime, I can at least understand your anger toward him. But why kill your uncle and then kidnap your mom and sister?"

Kyle let out a loud laugh, but not a laugh that follows a raucous joke, but an awkward laugh that tells you that you got it all wrong.

"It wasn't my dad that was abusing me," Kyle yelled. "It was my mom! You're just as dumb as the cops when I was a kid."

Wayne and Simon stared in silence. It was Isobella who was the one who beat Kyle.

"My dad never laid a hand on me or my sister and for some crazy reason, he loved Isobella so much that he didn't want her to be taken away. He let everyone think he was the bad guy and tried to protect everyone. Just so we could stay together. He said he would do anything to keep his family together."

"And in the end, he ended up living alone and losing everyone he cared about," Wayne said.

"Yeah," Kyle said. "Yeah."

And then with the truth finally in the open, he no longer had a façade he needed to hide behind. He dropped his head to where his arms were resting on the table and let out a deep painful shriek.

CHAPTER 46

Kyle's court case was quick, painful, and highly charged. A myriad of emotions flooded out, and they all came from those he left behind in the wake of his destruction.

Guilt. From the many people in Lake Pines who spent decades hating Sebastian and thinking he was a horrible man, when in fact, he was just trying to hold the people he cared about together.

Pain. From the Bernards who grew to love Devon in the short time that he lived with them and planned to offer him a life full of a loving family and a bright future, with the realization that their dream was stolen from them and that Devon didn't choose to walk away from them.

Remorse. From Isobella who came to realize far too late that her actions of anger had far-reaching repercussions than she could ever have imagined.

And that of hubris and how it can lead many an investigation down the wrong path with an incorrect and foregone conclusion when you don't have all the facts.

If Kyle had displayed the calmness in life that he had during his trial, lives may have been spared, but that was not the case.

Kyle accepted the charges, pleaded guilty, and as he waived a trial, began his sentence a short while later.

Kerry chose to not attend Kyle's court case. She had experienced enough of the damage he caused and didn't want to sit through another rendition of his crimes.

After Kyle was arrested, Isobella contacted Tom Pruitt and backed out of the sale of Crow Island with him. She had decided that it should remain with the rightful owner. Her daughter Katrina. And hoped that this one small act of contrition would be a step closer to repairing their relationship.

Today was the day she promised Simon that she would give him an answer about the dog, and she preferred to focus on that instead.

She waited on a blanket in the park at the edge of the main dock. The weather was warm and sunny, and the autumn season was panning out to be warmer than July, which was good since Kerry decided to take a much-needed few days off with Simon.

She had packed a lunch and planned to meet Simon at noon where she would be waiting in their favorite spot with the dog. She spotted Simon walking across the street and waved to him. He nodded his head but did not raise his hand to her.

The puppy began to jump and cry at the sight of Simon and it clawed at Kerry's arm as it tried to run to him.

Simon plopped down on the blanket and grabbed the dog, "Hey pup, I missed you too."

The dog began to lick Simon's face and he laughed at the feel. Kerry knew she lost any battle she was trying to fight, and in that instant, she wondered why she was fighting at all.

"So?" Simon asked.

"So?" Kerry teased.

"Do we keep him?"

"Yeah, we keep him," Kerry laughed.

Simon leaned over and kissed her, "Have you thought of a name for him?"

Kerry paused to think and just at that instant a large crow landed on the ground in front of them and walked close to where they sat, bobbing his head as he stepped. The puppy sat back and with its ears perked up let out a sequence of barks to which the crow flapped its wings and cried out before flying off.

Kerry turned to Simon, "How about Raven?"

Simon grabbed Kerry's hand, "Raven is a perfect name."

CHAPTER 47

Brian and Sibyl Bernard gathered Devon's belongings that they had saved in the small cardboard box. They stayed on the top shelf in the back of Sibyl's bedroom closet, untouched and unmoved for fifteen years. The box remained that way until Kerry and Simon arrived with the devastating news that Devon was believed to be the killer that they were searching for.

When they had left the Bernards' home, Sibyl broke down in tears. She fell into Brian's arms and he held her for the next half hour as she sobbed uncontrollably and in complete disbelief. There was no way, she asserted, that Devon could have become the monster that they described. He was a gentle child with a kind heart, and he had already lost so much that she knew he understood the pain it carried. Devon dreamed of a peaceful home and did his best to fit in and help with the two other foster children that the Bernards had living with them at the time.

But Sibyl grew anxious as Devon was quickly approaching the age where he would no longer be the responsibility of the foster care system. She worried that he would be forgotten, or worse, feel like he was no longer loved.

That's when Sibyl approached her husband about adopting Devon, "I want to make it official. Devon is our son in every imaginable way possible and I want him to know that he belongs with us. Forever."

Sibyl remembered her husband whisking her up in his arms as she imagined he always would upon receiving news that they were expecting. Which she never was. They never were able to conceive a child of their own, but quickly found the family they needed in Devon.

Once they were sure the paperwork could be put in quick motion for the adoption, they told Devon about their plans. They hoped that Devon felt the same, and as he dove into their arms, they knew that he did.

Then he disappeared.

They had always prayed he'd return to them, just not this way.

With the revelation that Devon was not the murderer, but Kyle's first victim, Sibyl, and Brian could prepare to finally bring their son home.

Kerry and Simon arrived at the cemetery just as the Bernards drove through the gate behind the white hearse carrying the remains of Devon Kozlowski.

Devon's complete remains were eventually found after extra manpower was deployed to the mudslide for another search, and he was prepared to be laid to rest.

The Bernards decided against cremation and wanted Devon to be buried in their family plot in Lake Pines.

Sibyl told Kerry, "*He was our son in all the ways that mattered, and he deserves to have a peaceful place to rest where we can visit him and remember the sweet soul he was. We at least owe him that.*"

Kerry glanced across the field and watched as the procession of three cars rounded the path and came to a stop near the north end of the cemetery.

As far as autumn days go, the day was exceptional. The warmth in the air settled down around them and carried the sweet smell of the nearby apple trees. Leaves had started to change color and one by one, they slowly fluttered to the ground.

A carpet of red, yellow, and orange illuminated the hill where the cemetery was located and within a few weeks, the grass would be completely covered. The fresh chill of the morning air had quickly warmed and the mourners that arrived to lay Devon to rest began to peel their coats from their shoulders and leave them behind in their cars.

Sibyl had insisted upon a white casket. She wanted to remember him as he was. An innocent child that was taken far too soon.

Kerry and Simon stood behind the Bernards, their friends, family, and the foster children they currently cared for.

Father Francis lead the group to the location where Devon was to be laid to rest. The polished casket was pulled from the back of the white hearse by four men. All dressed in dark suits and wearing matching orange ties. Devon's favorite color was orange. They carried the coffin twenty feet and rested it on the brass platform that was braced over the grave.

The reflection of the bright blue sky on the top of the polished casket and the colorful leaves that surrounded the cemetery brought a lightness to the somber event.

Father Francis read from a passage in his bible and spoke briefly about Devon's life and the short time he spent with the Bernards who grew to love him as they would their own son.

Brian Bernard then stood and began to speak. As his voice quivered, Sibyl grabbed hold of his hand. He steadied his voice and spoke.

Kerry couldn't recall the exact words he spoke, but the briefness was no indication of the amount of love that Devon brought into their lives, and that the Bernards had hoped they gave him in return.

Everyone stood as Devon's body was lowered into the ground and Kerry watched as Brian placed his shaking hand onto the casket as it was lowered into place.

Inside with Devon, was his baseball glove and a picture of his parents. And tucked next to his body was the envelope granting a formal adoption to the Bernards which arrived a week after he disappeared. The week after he died.

His name was carved with gold lettering into the gray headstone.

Devon Kozlowski-Bernard.

THE END

Author's Note

Thank you for reading, and I sincerely hope you enjoyed Murder Of Crows, the third book in the Lake Pines Mystery Series. Please check out the other books in the Lake Pines Mystery Series.

For a chance to win a free book, sign up at:
www.llabbott.com/book-giveaway

Every month there's a new contest and every name on my email list is entered to win. Over and over and over again. Plus, you'll be the first to know about new releases or sales. Your personal information will never be divulged, shared, or sold. If you're on social media. . . I would love to have you follow along.

Thanks again, my best to you and yours.
L.L. Abbott

Books by L.L. Abbott

Mystery & Suspense

Thrillers

Teen & Young Adult

General Fiction

Made in the USA
Monee, IL
01 December 2021

83640512R00177